Sleeping
with
the
Enemy

Janae Marie

My Warning: Prologue

I was a narcissistic bastard, born with an infectious disease that proved to have no cure. Condemned to a life of utterly shameless hell and torture. Figured I'd take as many people down for the ride with me. No fun in being alone. Every day seemed to be a new adventure as I sought out new victims to feed on. Too bad these ignorant souls could not see that I was truly the devil, alive on earth. Ready to steal, kill and destroy. Women love to buy me things and do whatever with me. I don't stop them because hell, what man wouldn't like that shit. But where some women usually fail with me...they don't focus on the inside. All women see when they are with me is this fine ass face and how I pleasure them. I am an addiction to most. Once I get inside you, I never leave. You are stuck with me forever. I don't mind at first but after a few years, I start to do damage to the body and tear down the morality of your soul and self–esteem. No one wants to live with me, yet they won't protect themselves from me. Do I feel bad about what I do to people, hell no.

People are responsible for their own actions. We are a part of an ignorant society where carelessness reigns supreme. We play ourselves repeatedly just for an hour or two of satisfaction.

We don't care about the repercussions of our actions. I remember a saying I once heard, "If looks could kill." I laugh at the mere thought. Because sometimes, they do.

Before I reveal to you everything about me; I must take you back to where all the chaos started and explain to you how I ended up in the place I am now. I'll begin with my life in high school where things began to get crazy, but I must tell you my story.

I sometimes like to torture those who don't care about the feelings of others. People are so selfish and thoughtless it makes me sick to my stomach.

The total lack and disregard to humanity is sickening.

Part I

Chapter 1

My Story

I was posted up by my locker waiting on my English class to start when I saw Melissa Owens, the finest chick at Chadsey School. She walked past me every day. She was perfection everywhere physically, her titties, ass, and hips but she also was a complete bitch. Melissa was the meanest and most stuck up girl I'd ever met. All that beauty mostly went to her head because she walked around like she was all that. I'd like to beat the shit of her for messing with my little sister, Geneva too.

"Hey, Geneva, where did you get that shirt from? I really like it."

"Thanks."

"Yeah, I liked it when it came out last season. Damn, why are you so poor? I feel so bad for you.

Hell, if it weren't for your brother, I'd feel sorry for you," she said laughing as she walked away.

Melissa made her way over to me. I played it cool like I always did. I let the hoes come to me

like they always do with their stupid asses.

1

"Hey Jeff, what's up? You look good today."

"What? Today? I look good every day. But why you always bagging on my sister, that shit ain't cool, Melissa."

"Okay, I'll stop. But I can't believe you two are related. You're so different."

"What's up with you and me?" I asked as I pulled her closer to me by the waist and stared deep into her eyes.

"I don't know. What is up with us? That's your call. What are you doing after school?"

"You, if you let me?" I said to her.

I couldn't believe how fast girls ate this shit up, I mean, damn, all I said was what are you doing after school and the bitch was putty in my hands.

"What time you free?"

"I'm free whenever you are, Ms. Melissa. Just one thing I have to know; my place or yours?" I whispered into her ear.

"We can do it at my place; I don't live that far away from here."

"Alright. Just hit me up after your last class."

"I sure will."

"Alright, Sweetie. I look forward to it." I said as I gave her a little pat on the behind. She looked back at me and smiled as she walked away to class. My sister walked right up to me and punched me lightly in the chest.

"What, Geneva?"

"How can you mess around with her after the way she treats me?"

"Stop worrying. I put a stop to all that. You won't have to worry about her messing with you anymore after I'm done with her ass tonight."

"Jeffrey, please tell me you're not going to do what I think you are?"

"What's that?" I laughed.

"You can't!"

"And pass up on that phat ass. I don't think so, Little Sis! But trust me; she won't be the same after being with me."

"You are a mess! You are talking about...you are going to..."

"Shh! Everybody doesn't need to know. Aren't you late for class, Sweetheart."

"You lucky, I'll see you at home."

"Alright, order something. You can't cook!" I yelled out.

"Shut up!"

I loved my sister, she was the only one that meant anything to me. Nobody else mattered. I didn't give a fuck about anything or anyone. My pops already scarred me for life so why would I care about the thoughts and feelings of others and I just hated selfish people who messed with mine.

I finally made my lazy ass way over to my English class, but Mr. Pratt was late, so I decided to catch up with a few of my boys who were in the class with me.

"Hey, Jeff, Man, I heard you were down with Melissa Owens. Man! Do you know about her?"

"What, that she fine as fuck?"

"Naw man, she out there. She'll do it to just anybody I heard," Bryant said.

"Shit, probably true, Man. Look at the body on her. You can't tell me ol' girl ain't been around the block but she ain't gon' know what to do once she's done with me."

"I feel you on that one, Man," my friend Scott said.

My teacher finally made it in talking about how he was running late because he had a flat tire or some shit. I was half listening. I was thinking about nailing Melissa's fine red bone ass. I couldn't wait to get her alone.

Later that day, I met Melissa at her locker talking to a couple of friends. I tapped her on the shoulder, and she was surprised that I was standing in front of her.

"You ready?"

"Oh yeah, I am ready."

"You change your mind or something?"

"No, I just thought you were going to back out."

"No, I thought you were going to back out. Hello, Ma," I said to her friend Jennifer, a short little brown skin cutie. She wanted to be like Melissa so bad. I could tell she wanted me too. Maybe once I was done with Melissa, I'd bone her friend.

"Alright, I'll talk to you later, Jennifer."

"Alright. Call me later, Girl!"

Melissa just smiled and turned. She put her arm around my waist and kissed me on the cheek. This girl just didn't know what she was doing to me. I was ready to take her right then. We walked to Melissa's car and she drove us over to her place.

Melissa had a nice home in a quiet little suburban neighborhood. She was a spoiled kid who got whatever the hell she wanted. Right now, she wanted me, and I was about to let her have it.

"So where are your parents at?"

"At work, of course. They don't come home until midnight."

"Mmhm, I like the sound of that. Look at y'all got flat screens and entertainment systems. I'm gon' have to challenge you on that X-box!"

4

"Naw, I'm pretty good at that. I'll kill you in some Madden."

"Whatever. But we both know this ain't what we came here for. So why are we stalling?"

"My bedroom is in there," she said, pointing to a closed door. "Come on."

She didn't waste any time heading to the room. We locked the door just in case. I lay out on the bed then she climbed right on top of me.

"Why do you want to be with me? There are so many girls in our school."

Because you're easy, damn! Why do girls always kill shit by talking? Just let me nut and get the fuck on shit! I got other things to see and other people to do. Yeah, I meant what I said.

"I like you. You know that. Melissa, you know you're the prettiest girl in that school. Why you even ask a question like that?" I said as I started to gently caress her thighs and her ass. She leaned into me and began kissing me passionately. She rubbed her hand up and down my chest and suddenly made its way to my dick. This girl was a true freak! I knew what everybody was saying about her was true. I couldn't believe how forward she was. The way she grabbed hold of me and told me how she wanted me to do her. I knew it would be on.

I thought about asking if the bitch if she had protection, but what the hell. If she don't say shit, I won't say shit either. I was ready to pound her ass so I could go back to my boys and tell them how good it was to be with Melissa Owens. I flipped her over and started feeling in between her legs. Women love that shit, love getting that pussy wet. I took pleasure and hearing the moans come from her as she grabbed on to my shoulders. I began to undress her and was pleased at what I saw. My hands rubbed against her D size chest. I was going to lick this girl out. I finished undressing and was ready to lay the pipe down on this broad. I pushed her down on the bed gently, looked deep into her eyes and entered her warm, moist pussy. This shit never felt so good. What felt even better was listening to her moan my name repeatedly. Only, if she knew what she was about to get from me. Repeatedly, I penetrated her and enjoyed every minute of it, making her cum numerous times. After, I released my deathly venom in this trick, she motioned for me to take the subway. I happily obliged. This silly girl just didn't know what I was going to do to her.

Melissa screamed my name repeatedly as she grabbed hold onto me. The way she yelled and kicked as she squirmed all over the bed was the highlight of all of this. Creating a water fall in between Melissa's legs made me want to enter her again. Apparently, she was surprised that I would do just about everything with her because I was tearing that ass up. I bust my fourth nut and called it a night. It was getting late anyway. I'd been over there for like five almost six hours. She looked worn out anyway. I kissed her on the cheek and started to put back on my clothes.

"Are you alright, Melissa?"

"Yeah, I just wasn't expecting all of that!"

"Well, now you can tell all of your friends how good my dick is."

"Whatever!"

Because best believe, I'm going to tell mine how good your pussy was.

"I'll call you, Mel. Don't have wet dreams about me!"

"Shut up! Alright goodbye, Jeff. I'll see you tomorrow."

I walked home from Melissa's house which wasn't much farther from where I lived. I felt good after fucking Melissa. I felt bad for her, but she probably deserved it. I hope my sister made something to eat because I was starving. We didn't stay with our parents; we were on our own. My father is doing life in prison for murdering our mother. Yeah, it's a pretty fucked up life. Luckily for Geneva, she has a different father from me. I was glad she was adopted and wasn't a bastard like me. She deserved better than the life that I had. I walked into the house and smelled the faint smell of spaghetti and garlic bread.

"Hey, Geneva. What's up?"

"What the hell are you doing coming home so damn late, it's eleven thirty?"

"I told you, I was with Melissa!"

"What? Jeffrey, don't you ever feel bad about what you do to these girls?"

"No! Why should I feel bad? She wanted to fuck me. Damn, I should've made her suck my dick!"

"J! Come on!"

"Why do you care so much about her? She treats you like shit?"

"But she still doesn't deserve to be given a death sentence."

"Look, what do you want me to do 'Neva? There is nothing I can do. What do you want me to do, not have sex?"

"Yes!"

"I didn't do this to myself, it happened to me. I'm not going to stop something I enjoy just because of some fucked up shit. I like sex. Hell, I love sex. So, leave me alone. I'm hungry. Where is the food at?"

"It's in the microwave. I'm going to bed."

"Goodnight!"

7

I knew my sister worried about me. But I was seventeen years old going on eighteen. I was all she had. I had to deal with some horrific shit because my father was out there. How the hell is that my fault. If I could, I'd go to that prison and beat the shit out his ass. I hope I don't end up in there with him one day. Right now, I enjoyed pussy and the feeling I got from having sex. I had no plans on stopping anytime soon.

The next day at school, I was standing outside of the building waiting on the homeroom to begin when Bryant and Scott approached me, wondering how my one-night stand went with Melissa.

"I know you uh, put it down on her right!" Scott asked.

"Man, what you think? She was exhausted after I bust for the fourth time," I said as they all began to laugh.

"Shh, there she is," I said as Melissa made her way toward the door with a few of her friends.

"Hey, what's up, Jeffrey?"

"What's up, Baby. How are you doing?"

She continued in the building as we stood outside. Melissa and her friends walked over to the cafeteria to grab some breakfast before class started.

"So, Girl, come on and tell me how it was! I know that Jeffrey is so good looking!" Jennifer asked, she was more like a follower of Melissa.

"Wait, did I miss something?" Nadia questioned.

"I had sex with Jeffrey last night!"

"What? Are you serious?"

"Yes, Girl! Let me tell you! His penis is so big! He knows exactly what to do with it too! I mean, we did it repeatedly. He went down on me to, Girl! I mean, we did just about everything last night. I am telling y'all, he is good. I got to have him again."

Geneva happened to be walking past and heard Melissa talking about the rendezvous she had. She walked up to her trying to get her attention.

"Uh, Melissa, I need to tell you something."

"What the fuck would you need to tell me, Loser!" she asked, as her friends begin to cackle with laughter.

"Look, I know you don't like me, but I seriously need to tell you something. It's about my brother."

"I already know everything there is to know about your fine ass brother. Girl, did I tell you that he lasted for almost six hours! I mean whoa! I was exhausted!"

"Melissa, I don't mean to be nosey, but did you happen to use a condom with my brother?"

"What, why, I'm on the pill. He ain't gon' get me pregnant? And damn, why the fuck are you still here all up in my business! Get away from me!"

"You know what? You are a bitch, Melissa, and you deserve what my brother just gave you!"

"What, bitch? Who the hell you calling a bitch? I'll kick your ass!"

"Hey, Melissa, calm down," Nadia said, trying to deescalate the situation.

"I don't know what the hell her problem is!"

"Hey, I think I should be heading to the library now. I have to print out a paper before I go to class," Jennifer mentioned.

"Alright, goodbye Jennifer. See you later," Melissa commented.

"But don't you think she might have been trying to tell you something about him? And why the hell didn't you use protection? I mean, I know he is finer than no other, but don't you think that he probably sleeps around? A lot of girls like him, Melissa."

"So, that don't mean he sleeps with them. I got tested two months ago and I'm clean. Please stop worrying about me. Let's get ready for class."

Melissa and Nadia made their way out of the cafeteria, but Geneva still wanted to warn Melissa. She pulled her by the arm and whispered in her ear.

"My brother has…"

"What? What is it that you need to tell me about him so damn bad?"

"Look, all I can say is you might want to watch yourself around him. He isn't who you think he is."

"All I can say is you need to leave me alone. I am with him and I don't need you trying to persuade me to leave him. Leave me alone, damn!" she said as she walked out of the cafeteria.

Some people just didn't have any disregard for anything. Now later, when she finds out what's really going on, she'll blame Geneva for not warning her. But by then, it'll be too late. I spent six hours pleasuring her sweet body, but it took only six minutes to destroy her sweet little body.

Chapter 2

The Spread

It was another boring ass day of school and I couldn't wait to get the hell out of there. I ran into my friend Stacy in the hallway as I searched for my geometry book in my locker. Stacy tapped me on the shoulder to get my attention.

"What's up, Jeff? How you doing? What you got up later today?"

"Shit, what are you doing?"

"Nothing. How about you come over and chill with me later today?"

"Sure, that's cool, Stacy."

"Hey, why don't you come out to Club Tonic on Friday? They're throwing a party. It's supposed to be banging!"

"Alright, sounds good to me. Hey, let's get out of here."

I wasn't feeling that math class, so I hopped in the car and went back to Stacy's place. Stacy had a nice place. *I always pick the ones with money. I like for people to give me shit. Yeah, I'm a piece of shit. I know. But hey, what can I say? It's the life of a playa!*

We started to get things popping. I didn't like to wait around. Stacy and I had

been messing around since our freshmen year and we were now going into our senior year.

Stacy was always willing to do whatever whenever. I liked that. There wasn't any questions asked. We did what we had to do and moved on to the next thing. Stacy dropped down in front of me; and began to unbutton my pants, slowly pulling out my penis and began sucking on it like a chocolate lollipop. I grabbed the back of Stacy's head and enjoyed the hell out of that shit. Nobody sucked me that good. The tighter I grabbed; the harder Stacy sucked. I could feel myself getting ready to explode. I came all over Stacy as I bust my nut.

The shit had never felt so good, so I had to return the favor.

Stacy walked over to the bedroom and bent over the desk and I started fucking from the back. I could tell that Stacy was feeling that shit just as much as I was, moaning at every deep stroke I gave. In and out, in and out. I enjoyed giving it and I knew Stacy enjoyed giving it to me. Too bad, we had to keep what we did on the down low. Stacy was one of the best partners I ever had. After I bust my third nut, I got dressed and headed for home. I fell right asleep once I got to my bedroom. I slept well that night. The next day, I was at my locker getting my books for chemistry class when I saw Stacy walking down the hallway.

"Hey, Stacy, come here for a minute!"

"Yeah? What's up, Jeff?"

"Who is that girl I been seeing you with all day?"

"Uh, she is my girlfriend."

"Hey, Stacy. I didn't know you had a girlfriend. How long you been dating her?"

"Since sophomore year and why wouldn't I have a girlfriend? I have a reputation to uphold. I am the captain of the football team. Come on, Man!"

"Look," he said to me quietly. "I know that we've been messing around for quite a while now. But it was you that wanted to keep this on the down low. Am I right? "

"Yeah, I just..."

"Trust me; nothing is going to change between us. Now let me tend to my girl before she starts to get upset. I'll catch up with you later. And oh, don't forget, that party this weekend!"

Stacy walked over to his girlfriend Veronica and gave her a kiss on the cheek. After all the years I'd known Stacy, I sure as the hell didn't know this nigga had a motherfucking girlfriend. This shocked the hell out me. I couldn't believe Stacy would put his girlfriend at risk just because of his stupid ass reputation. *Just like a nigga!* Now this nigga infected and his girl and she didn't even ask for it.

Chapter 3

The Party

The day of the Tonic Nightclub party finally came, and I was truly ready to get my party on. It had been a long time since I'd let loose and just enjoyed myself. Me and my boys walked through the club and saw a plethora of beautiful women. Tonic was on fire. There was nowhere in the building that wasn't jumping. The DJ was playing all the jams. I began to scope the room and I saw Stacy and Veronica surrounded by several other people from the football team.

I decided to walk over and see how they were doing.

"Hey, what's up, Stacy?"

"Oh, what's up? Man, how you doing? Glad you could make it out tonight, Jeffrey!" he said as he turned his back to continue to chat with the other members of the football team.

"You want to pretend you don't know who I am now?" I asked him quietly.

"Hey, who is your friend, Stacy?" his girlfriend Veronica cut in.

"Oh, this is Jeffrey. You want to dance, Babe?"

"Sure, it was nice meeting you Jeffrey." She respectfully stated.

"Yeah. It was nice meeting you too. Hey, Stacy?"

"What?"

"I think if you ask me, you could do a lot better, Man." I whispered to him as he walked on the dance floor to be with his girl. I thought about how big of a punk bitch he was. He did not have the fucking courtesy to tell his girl he was on the down low. This nigga literally didn't know who he was dealing with. The worse part of it all was that he tried to blow me off and did not even have the balls to look me in the face. He could have at least played the shit off. If I were a hatin' ass nigga, I could have exposed all his dirty little laundry, but I decided to keep my cool and do what I'd came to do. I walked back toward where my fellas Scott and Bryant were standing by the bar.

"Hey, do y'all know if Nina is here?" I asked.

"Why do you want to know if she's here?" Scott questioned.

"Man, because she's fine as hell, Scott, why did you even ask me that? Bitch looking like Nicki Minaj and shit."

"Yeah, I heard she is a freak just like her too. Man, I already saw at least five dudes she already had sex with."

"Man, I don't give a... Scott, do you know who I am? I'm about to go find her. I'll be right back.

I searched the entire floor for Nina's fine freaky ass. I didn't give a damn about how many other dudes she was with. I was about to get it in with her for sure. I walked past a group of fine ladies heading over to the VIP. I called out for Nina and she turned around quickly and walked over to me.

"Damn, Jeffrey I didn't know you were bringing your fine ass to the party. What's up?"

"Shit! I was looking for you."

"Well, you found me. I was about to head to the VIP with my girls but now that I saw you. I might have to change those plans."

"You want to dance?"

"Hell yeah!"

I was relieved to have found Nina. She was a little freak true; but like I said earlier.

What guy is going to pass up a fine ass girl like this? The DJ turned on Usher's, "OMG" and this girl started getting loose on me. Nina was backing that ass up on me, making my dick hard as shit! I couldn't wait to go to work on this girl's pussy. I grabbed her by the waist and whispered in her ear how bad I wanted to do her. She told me that we could do whatever.

After the song ended Nina led me to the women's restroom. Luckily, it was empty. I watched as she locked the door behind her and started to take off her top. She slowly walked toward me, running her hand down my chest. I could feel the veins in my dick begin to pulsate. Nina moved my head down her chest and motioned for me to go to work on her size double D chest. I massaged her nipples then sucked the shit out her titties until she begged me to stop. I pushed Nina against the wall and pulled down her pants.

I placed both of her legs on my shoulders as I kneeled and proceeded to eat her out. As my tongue entered her warm sweet pussy, I could feel her squirm and grab hold to me. The tighter she grabbed, the harder I sucked on her clit. The walls of her pussy were like a waterfall, and I was ready to take stream. I enjoyed my late-night snack. There was nothing like the taste and feel of being in some wet ass pussy. Nina finally exploded and I rose up as I wiped the sides of my mouth. I took one look at her and thought about how bad I truly wanted to fuck her. I immediately pulled out my eight-inch steel and wrapped her legs around my waist. I entered her, still soaking wet. I penetrated her and could feel that she was truly enjoying this shit. She planted gentle kisses on my neck as I continued to hold her up and rub her fat ass. I never knew being with Nina Coleman was so good. She had the type of pussy that kept you coming back. I'd have to get some from her again. Now I knew what the other dudes was talking about. The harder Nina moaned my name the harder and faster I fucked her; I started banging her faster and faster against the wall. Thus, making the screams much more rapid; I was surprised nobody come knocking at the door.

Damn, I thought, *I haven't had a good fuck like this since Melissa.* After we both came, Nina grabbed a hold of me breathing heavily. I stared into her eyes and kissed her on the lips. I fixed myself up and left the bathroom. I hadn't felt that good in a long time. I went back to the party and even danced with a few girls. By the end of the night, I had forgotten all about what his name...Stacy?

The next week at school, everyone was talking about how good that party was. I was just getting out of class when I was telling my two best friends how good Nina's pussy was that night. We were all standing by the gym about ready to shoot some hoops. I continued to tell them the story as I saw Veronica and her nosy ass friend Bethany across the room.

"Hey Veronica, I need to tell you something about your little boyfriend. I think you might want to sit down for this one."

"Oh, god. What are you talking about now?"

"Now I could be wrong, but I really think I should tell you this tidbit of info that I heard. I mean I really don't want to hurt you, but I think I should tell you, me being your best friend and all."

"Damn, will you just tell me already?"

"Okay, well you know how my locker is about a couple of lockers down from Jeffrey's right?"

"Yes, I know. Y'all are in the same homeroom."

"Well, what I'm about to tell you will truly shock you, Girl!"

"Well, what is it already?"

"I think Stacy is messing around with Jeffrey!"

"What?"

"Look, I heard him telling Stacy about how they use to mess around. I'm sorry but I'm only going by what I heard, and I am sure of what I heard."

Veronica didn't waste any time with this little bit of information. She searched the entire school until she found Stacy who happened to be in the boy's locker room. Veronica burst through the doors screaming his name.

"Stacy! Stacy? Stacy Monroe!"

"Girl, what the hell is you doing in here? You know you're not supposed to be in here."

"We need to talk! Follow me!" she said as she pulled him over to the side where the showers were.

"Um...I heard from Bethany that you were messing around with that guy we met at the party. Now is that true or not?"

"What? She sounds stupid as hell."

"Just tell me the truth, Stacy!"

"She is just making up shit because she jealous of you and she wants to be with me. Hell, maybe she wants to be with you. I don't know. Why would you believe that crazy shit?" he asked, wiping his bare chest with a towel and walking away from her.

She began to call out to him, but he didn't turn around. She walked out of the locker room and began to search for me.

19

Veronica found me in my usual hang out spot. I was sitting on a bench, playing with some apps on my iPhone. She decided to sit right next to me. Her eyes looked kind of puffy as if she had been crying.

"Please tell me the truth?"

"Tell you the truth about what, Veronica?"

"Have you been sleeping with my man?"

"What the hell? I'm not a fag, what type of shit...Girl, what the hell are you even talking about? What do you think? What did he tell you?"

"He told me not to believe it."

"Well, then don't believe...Why in the hell why would I sleep with a dude? Come on, Veronica," I told her as I walked away and headed home.

****

It was a pretty warm day, so I decided to sit on the porch and enjoy the little cool breeze that blew past every now and again. I didn't know what was going to happen between Stacy and Veronica but I was sure everybody was going to be talking about it.

"Jeffrey!" My sister called me from the house.

"Yeah, I'm outside."

"What the hell is going on? So, are the rumors true?"

"You want to know if I..."

"Was with Stacy?" she completed my sentence.

"Look, there are people in that school that love to make things up."

"So, you admit it? Are you gay?"

"Hell no, I'm not gay. Why would you ask me that?"

"I'm confused... What are you then?"

"I'm living life...That's what I'm doing."

"You're infecting harmless people. I mean, did you forget your ailment?"

"Look, Geneva, I can't ever forget what I have. But I can't just stop living my life. I got to be

me and do what I want. What do you want me to do? Sit around and be depressed? Feel sorry for myself?"

"I don't know...I just don't know anymore," she said as she walked back into the house.

I sat back down and opened a bag of Cheetos that I had lying on the porch next to me. As I popped the chips into my mouth, I saw Melissa Owens walking down the street. She looked like she was walking toward my house.

"Jeffrey, I need to talk to you!"

"Melissa, what's up?"

"I'm pregnant!"

"What?"

Chapter 4

A Harsh Reality

"You heard me, Jeffrey! You got me pregnant."

"I didn't get you pregnant! Girl, you know just as well as me that you slept around with damn near every brother at that school. So why the hell are you blaming this shit on me?"

"What? You were the last guy I slept with, so I know you got me pregnant. Just face it. It was you."

"Get the fuck out of here, Melissa, with that shit. I know I didn't bust one in you. So please get on with that garbage. You need to leave my house and go find your baby daddy."

"You are such an ass. If you want to take a DNA test, we can."

"What are you talking about? You can't get a DNA test until the baby gets here. And by the time a baby gets here, I won't even be around. You are wasting my time, like I said; you need to find your baby daddy. Oh, and by the way, you might want to go head to the clinic while you're at it! You're going to get a big surprise."

Melissa stormed off my porch in a frustrated frenzy. I was pretty sure I had gotten her pregnant. But did I care, no. Did I want to be a part of its life, hell no! She made her bed and now she had to lie in it. I didn't want or need any damn kids right now. How the hell could I be a good father with my type of medical condition. I wouldn't want an innocent ass kid being put through that kind of torture like I was. At least I gave a damn about how my kids are or might be affected by this shitty ass disease. My father didn't give a flying fuck. But that's the reason why he is where he is right now. I decided that all this was just way too much to deal with. So, I took my ass to sleep for a couple of hours, just to take my mind off things.

****

A couple of weeks later, Melissa did take herself down to the clinic to see what she would do about her baby. She looked around frantically as she waited for the doctor to call her into the room for her lab results. She had been pregnant for about a few weeks. It was still early in her pregnancy and she didn't know what she was going to do. But when she talked to the doctor, she came up with an answer quickly.

The clinic was filled with women of all different races and ages. There were a few little kids playing and some crying. It was kind of a scary place to be alone, especially if you were experiencing an unplanned pregnancy. Finally, the doctor called Melissa into the private room to go over her recent lab work. She took a seat as the doctor closed the door and took a seat in front of her staring at the paperwork as if preparing to tell her the news.

"Well, Ms. Owens, I want to congratulate you on your recent pregnancy. But now I want to go over your lab work. You tested negative for, chlamydia, gonorrhea and syphilis but unfortunately, you did however test positive for HIV."

"What, are you serious?"

"Yes, now do you know who might've given you this disease?"

"Yeah, I'm sure I do."

"Now, you are still extremely early in your pregnancy. What I am about to say may or may not upset you. But you can still decide to terminate this pregnancy. I am not saying that you cannot have a healthy pregnancy, but you will have to take medication to prevent the disease from carrying over to and being produced in the child. If you take the medication you have a chance of lowering the baby's, chances of getting this illness to about twenty-five percent. Would you really want to put the child at such a horrific risk that the child could still get the disease through your breast milk? I'm not telling you to abort but it may be something to consider. I am going to prescribe some medication for you. You will have to take some pills to keep your immunity low, so it won't build up as quickly and attack your blood cells. I am sorry about this."

Melissa broke down and began to cry. She couldn't believe that this was happening to her. Life as she knew it was over. Melissa knew that she could never have a normal life again.

****

What will she do? How will she live with herself? How will she tell her friends, her family? What will she do about her baby? Should she just abort? It would be selfish for her to bring a child in this world that may have a chance of being sick for the rest of its life. I'm quite sure she knows I'm the one who gave her the disease, but she can't find it in herself to face the realness of this situation.

A couple of days later, Melissa stood by her locker balling in tears. Her best friend Nadia came up to her and noticed she was distraught. She attempted to console her by giving her a hug.

"Oh my God, what's wrong, Melissa? Do you want to talk about it?"

"Uh, no, I'll be fine. Thanks for asking though," she said through choked tears.

"What is it? Are you failing a class or something? Is it a family issue?"

"Don't worry about it, Nadia. I'll be fine."

"Alright, I'm going to head off to class now. I'll call you later, to check up on you, alright Girl! You'll be okay. See you, Melissa!"

"See you, Nadia."

Melissa waved goodbye to her friend and gathered herself to go to class. She spotted Geneva, grabbing her geography and mathematic textbooks from her locker. Melissa approached Geneva slowly and stared her in the eyes.

"I should've listened. I should've listened to you. You tried to warn me, now my life is over. I'm sorry; I wish I would have listened to you instead of being such a hard-headed bitch. Now my life is over!" she repeated.

"Melissa, what are you talking about?" Geneva asked as she closed her locker.

"Nothing, I have to go now. Just tell your brother that he is a horrible person and he deserves to rot in hell!"

"What happened?"

"I think you know what happened already!" Melissa yelled as she continued to walk down the hallway to class. Geneva stood there for a moment before leaving. At that moment, she knew something just wasn't right.

Later on, that day, Geneva arrived home, yelling out my name. I was in my room listening to some music, trying to relax until she burst in my room, messing up my groove.

"Damn, 'Neva. What do you want? I was trying to relax."

"What is Melissa talking about? She came up to me today. What did you do to her?"

I knew Melissa would say something eventually to my sister about her situation. I just wished she hadn't done it so soon. I sat up on my bed and lowered the headphones around my neck.

"I got Melissa Owens pregnant."

"What! You did what?" my sister shouted out as she took a seat at my desk.

"So, I'm pretty sure she knows she got that disease by now."

"And you don't feel bad about what you did to that girl?"

"Why the hell do you care? That girl used to pick with you every single day."

"That's not the point. She is an innocent human being and now she can never experience a normal adult life. She is going to be on medication for the rest of her life!"

"So what? Am I supposed to feel sorry for her or something?"

"You are supposed to think about your actions and how you are affecting others in this world. Jeff, please stop being so damn selfish. Think about others."

"Stop being selfish, think about others? What about me? No one is thinking about me. I don't know if you realized it or not, but there isn't a cure for this shit! Doctors don't give a damn about you. They push some pills your way and send you out the door. No one is going to feel sorry for me! So why in the hell should I ever feel sorry for them? I don't care who I hurt because I'm hurt! I'm hurt, Geneva! I don't have time to feel sorry for no damn body. At the end of the day, who the hell is going to feel sorry for me? Nobody, so do you really think I give a care about who the hell I give it to?"

"Wow!" Geneva got up and walked toward the living room.

"What, Geneva?"

"You are a murderer!"

"Oh, I'm a murderer? What about the sick fuck who gave me the disease? That nigga somewhere locked up in solitary confinement in Jackson Prison. My daddy messed my life up and who the hell...is going...to pat me on the back and let me know that everything is going to be okay? Nobody!"

I strained to hold back the tears that began to fall from eyes. This was the first time in about seventeen and a half years that my condition really emotionally affected me. I mean, it was the truth; I didn't have anybody in my life that could relate to my situation. Therefore, I was the way I was. I don't have any sympathy for anyone. I never saw the reason to. No one had or will have sympathy for me. It's a dog eat dog world out here.

"I feel sorry for you. I really wish that I could do something. I mean I understand-"

"No! You will never 'understand' how the hell I feel or what I'm going through until you are living with the disease yourself. Other than that, Geneva, you will never know what it feels to be HIV positive."

I wiped the tears away from my face as my sister gave me a huge hug. I hadn't had a sympathetic hug in a long time. It felt good for someone to care about how I felt. I did so much to protect my little sister. Although she was adopted, I still loved her the same. She was lucky though. Geraldine, my mother who now rests in peace, just wanted a daughter. Too bad for her she had to be brought into this crazy madness.

I went back to listening to music. I contemplated a lot of what was going on in my life. Maybe it wasn't too late to make some changes in my life. I don't know if I could keep living with the fact that I could be possibly infecting so many people. I knew just the person I had to see to get over this pain that I was feeling. I had to get some type of closure to all of this.

Chapter 5

The Visit

Looking around, I saw my father being trapped in a concrete jungle with murderers, pedophiles, rapist and whoever else was in this asylum. I hoped I never ended up in a place like that. Waking up from my trance, I saw Malik Willis, better known to me as my father standing right before me.

I didn't know how to feel. This man had never been in my life. Prison wasn't doing him any justice. He had salt and pepper hair and a few cuts and bruises on his face. His brown skin looked to have not been well managed. I suppose they really didn't take care of his medical condition. He sat down across from me and I stared in his eyes, wishing I could choke the living daylights out of him. He was the reason I was suffering. He was the reason why I'd never live a normal life.

"Well thank you for coming, Son. I really wanted to see you. You know my days are numbered here on this earth. I'm not going to be here much longer-"

"Man, miss me with all that sensitive emotional stuff. What are you, a female now? Too many sticks up the ass. What you call me here for?" I questioned him.

I didn't have any sympathy for him, nor did I want to listen to his sob stories.

"Don't make me fuck you up in here, Little Boy. I might be in lockdown, but I'll still kick your ass. Now I called you here to let you know I'm about to be executed in a few weeks and I just wanted to see you before you I'm gone."

"What the hell did you do?"

"I've been in solitary confinement for nine months. I've passed the HIV virus to over sixty people since I've been in the Jacksonville Correctional Facility. I'm going to get the electric chair for it."

I didn't know what the fuck to say to that. It was some pretty sinister shit.

"Just how did you get this shit in the first place?" I just had to know.

"Well, some years ago when I was just about your age, I didn't give a damn about protecting myself. Thought I was that dude who could talk any girl out her panties. Hell, I was putting in work. I didn't give a damn about none of these hoes. I was smashing like four, five girls a month or more. Thought I was invincible. Now for your mother, that bitch was weak. Didn't have a backbone. She didn't listen to me. Kept getting in my way. "

"So, you continued to beat her until you killed her! You're sick piece of shit. You ruined my fucking life. You might not have cared for your own life, but you certainly messed up mine. I ought to kick your fucking ass," I mouthed off toward my father.

My father stood up to whisper something to me.

"Stop being such a bitch ass pussy. No one gives a damn about you in this world. Think someone is going to have sympathy for you because you have this shit? Fuck no! Make these little fuckers feel what you feel. Why should you be the only one suffering? Think I felt bad for what I did to those people? Oh no. Now I'm going out in style. You're going to die anyway; you might as well take some people with you. Be remembered for something. Grow some balls boy!"

"That's fucked up, Malik."

"That's life. Get over it. Things don't always work the way you want them to."

While I listened to my father explain his reasoning, a guard walked over and said our time was up. He had to go back in the hole, and I had to leave. I got up from the table and as I made my way home, I couldn't get that message out my head.

Sadly, I had to say I agreed. Why should I be the only one suffering from this. It wasn't right for people to have gotten away with their promiscuous ways while others were forced to a life of ill health and being a social outcast. Maybe Geneva was right. I was slowly becoming just like my father. I'd passed on the virus to three or more people already. It wasn't right, but what could I do.

Chapter 6

Melissa

I couldn't believe this was now my reality. I knew I shouldn't have been with him. His sister tried to warn me. Why didn't I listen? How could he have given me this? He knew, he fucking knew! He ruined my life. I am a pregnant teen now living with HIV. What the fuck will I do now? My parents are strict as shit and I don't even know how to tell them this awful news. How will I face him at school? How will I face anyone at school? I can't even look at myself in the mirror. My life is over. I can't bring a child into this world. Not like this.

I walked into my house and couldn't get over it no matter how hard I tried. I listened to music, but nothing worked. I paced around the living room and grew angrier. I ran into the bathroom and vomited repeatedly. The sheer shock of this information had my stomach unsettled. As I attempted to stand up, I stared at my reflection. I was no longer the same person. A piece of me died. I felt no life inside of me. My life was ruined all because I wanted to have sex with a guy, I was interested in. There was nothing wrong with that. Jeffrey should have opened his mouth and told

35

me about his disease. He was a selfish bitch who only thought of himself. I hated him and I hated myself for allowing this to happen. The longer I stood at the mirror, the more I decided I couldn't take it anymore. I looked around the room and I picked up a small bag of rocks and threw them hard at the mirror until it broke. I punched walls repeatedly while blood dripped from my hands. I had to talk to him. I had to confront Jeffrey. I didn't know how my life would turn out because this was devastating. I'll never bounce back from this.

The next few days at school, after I finally summoned up the courage to return to school, I stood by my locker in tears when my best friend Nadia approached me, attempting to console me.

"Oh my god, Melissa. What's wrong? Why are you crying? Are you okay?"

"No, no, I'm fine! My life is ruined! I can't ever get over this."

"Do you want to talk about it?" Nadia asked.

"No, I don't want to talk about anything. I don't even want to be here! My life is over. Just leave me alone!" I cried as I walked away.

I began searching for Jeffrey. We had to talk. He had to know how I felt. He took away something so precious to me, I'd never get back.

Chapter 7

Jeffrey: A Hard Blow

The next day at school, I was retrieving my calculus textbook out of my locker when I got interrupted by Melissa Owens, staring at me angrily. I shut my locker door and turned to her to see what she wanted now.

"Yes, Melissa? What is it now?" I questioned.

"You! How could you do this to me? You knew, Jeffrey. You fucking knew!" she cried.

"What in the world are you talking about, Girl? I'm still not taking care of that baby that isn't
mine!"

"Oh, this is your baby! But I went to the doctor for a check-up and found out that I'm HIV positive. Jeffrey, you were the last person that I had sex with, and you know we didn't use condoms. So, don't even begin to play me like that. I ought to tell everybody up in this school about you."

"You could, but you won't because you're a little scary bitch. You would have to admit that you got this shit too. Little Miss Perfect Melissa Owens had unprotected sex. You don't want word to get out that you a ho who fucks without a condom and caught an incurable STD. Bitch please, you aren't gon' say shit!" I ranted back to her.

I knew I infected Melissa with this, and I was being an asshole but what could I do. She put herself out there. She should have been smarter. It's not my fault Melissa opted out of using condoms.

"What do you want me to do, Melissa? You got it now, ain't no getting rid of that baby! You wanted to be with me. You got what you wanted. Now if you don't mind, I'm running late for class. I got to go," I concluded rudely.

Tears began to roll down her cheeks. I grabbed my books and headed down the hallway. No sympathy was felt after talking to her. She treated my sister and a few other people in that school like shit. I guess in a way, she got what was coming to her. As I walked down the hall, I heard her cry out.

"I hate you, Jeffrey. I hate you. How could you do this to me? You ruined my life and you don't even care! I can't believe you gave me this!"

A week later, I was walking down the hallway and saw a few people crying and looking sad. I wondered what the hell was going on. Geneva found me standing by the auditorium. I pulled her over to the side to find out why everyone was being so glum.

"Hey, Geneva, what's going on? Did I miss something?"

"You haven't heard? Melissa Owens died!"

"What! Are you serious?" I couldn't believe what I was hearing.

"People are saying she was murdered. But I really believe that she killed herself. She was depressed. Nadia said she received a phone call from her parents who found her bloody body lying in her bedroom. You see, Jeffrey, you made that girl end her life. You ought to be so fucking proud of yourself. She was pregnant with your baby, and then found out she had an incurable disease. What the hell is wrong with you?"

"Her bloody body?"

"Yeah, she shot herself."

I couldn't believe what the hell I'd just heard. My heart sank into my chest. *No way this girl killed herself. Wow, this is some deep shit to process. I almost feel like a murderer because I'm the reason behind her choosing to end her life. Me and my asshole behavior behind what happened to her. What am I supposed to do? I have my life to live and I sure as hell can't spend mine, grieving about her. I feel bad for her parents, but oh well. Life surely does go on.*

I couldn't stand to be in that miserable place around all those depressed people. They were canceling classes anyway, so I just headed home. Then what I walked up on was even worse. I saw a couple of cars from the county parked right in front our house. I entered the house and saw our grandmother with a couple of White people, dressed in business entire. I knew nothing good would come from them. Geneva came in shortly after me.

"What's going on? How'd you guys get in here?" I asked.

"Well, Mr. Willis, we were permitted entry from the landlord. We're from the State, Child Protective Services. We found out that you lied on some documents to get yourself emancipated from the state. You are not yet of legal age which entails you be made a ward of the court. You, as well Geneva. But your grandmother has been nice enough to take her in. You however, Mr. Willis, will have to come with us and be placed into foster care until your eighteenth birthday," the White guy with the tailored blue suit said.

I couldn't believe it. There was no way in hell I wanted to go back to foster care. My birthday was in six months. This clearly didn't make any sense. It was just a way to split my sister and I up. I'd been taking care of that little girl since our grandmother walked out on us. I had to; we were all alone.

My father was in jail and well... my mother... died at the hands of his abusive ways. I began to get angry. I didn't care that this was my grandmother. This lady was crooked as hell.

"You know this is just a crock of shit, right? I have been taking care of her! You left us in this house because you didn't want to deal with us. Especially me. You came around every so often to take my money to keep for yourself. Now that you know the money is coming to a stop because I'm going to be an adult soon, you want to split us up so you can collect from Geneva. But—"

"Ain't nobody taking nothing from you. Watch your mouth when you talk to me. What you did was illegal. You ought to be thankful I didn't let them take you to jail. Now I'm going to take care of Geneva and provide her with a good life, better than the bull you've been offering. Your father cursed your life the day he shot you out his peter. And I'm not going to subject Geneva to a life full of damnation like yours."

My grandmother was a sneaky and conniving witch. She really was. She was supposed to take care of us after my father was sent to prison. The judge granted her full custody of us but once I got old enough to take care of myself; she left us. Every so often she'd come by, check on us and collect the money she'd get for taking us in and then leave us again. I vowed to Geneva that I'd never leave her. I'd taken care of her for years and now that I'm about to turn eighteen, she wants to take her away because the money is coming to an end.

"Geneva! I know you're not leaving with her?" I questioned her.

"I don't know what else to do here."

"Leave that girl alone. Come on, Geneva. We got to go. Bye, Jeffrey."

My grandmother left with my sister and I felt like my heart was being ripped from my chest. I watched her get in the car and drive off. I hoped that wouldn't be the last time I saw her. Geneva was the only person I truly loved on this earth. After she was taken from me, I honestly didn't care about anything or anyone. All I could do was get on with my life.

Part II: Eighteen Months Later

Chapter 8

Jeffrey: The Friend

I finally made it out of that institutional prison, just to enter another, better known as Harry S. Truman college. Just like high school, I was running things, I was the man. I had groupies everywhere, but one girl in particular named Octavia had taken a real liking to me. We'd been talking on and off for about five months when I moved in with her. Things were cool until she introduced me to her best friend, Cynthia. Octavia was a small petite girl but her friend Cyn, she was thick in all the right places. Where Octavia lacked, Cyn more than made up for. Hell, Octavia wasn't giving up the ass anyway, so I had to get it from somewhere.

It was around 2:30 in the afternoon and Octavia was just coming in the house.

"Hey Jeffrey! I want you to meet my home girl, Cynthia. She's going to be staying here for a few days while she's visiting from out of town."

"Well, look at you, Girl! You got yourself a cute one. He looks good girl!" Cynthia squealed excitedly.

I knew exactly what I would be getting from Cynthia. She gave me the look like she was ready to go to bed with me right there.

"Come on, Girl. You'll be staying in here," Octavia said as she led her to the extra room she converted into a bedroom.

A little later that day, Octavia went to work at the hospital which left me alone with Cynthia. I was sitting on the couch watching a television show. I saw Cynthia walking toward me wearing a tank top and short shorts, showing off her wonderful assets. This girl was not only a tease but a thot. Apparently, her friendship with Octavia meant nothing to her.

"Hey, J, what are you watching?" she questioned.

"Um, just a show on VH-1. So, how long you plan on staying here?" I questioned, making empty conversation, wondering what this girl had planned.

"For about a month. I just got offered a job out here. I'm staying until I get a place."

"How long have you known Octavia?"

"Um, for a while," she replied coyly as she began rubbing on my knee and then slowly made her way up my thigh.

This girl didn't even know me and was already trying to make moves on me. Hell, I wasn't going to stop her just because she was a little thot. Next thing I knew, shorty had her tongue in my mouth and her hands in my pants. Cynthia was very forward with me, she stopped kissing me and began blowing me off. I couldn't lie, the shit was feeling damn good. I hadn't had a blowjob in quite some time. I wanted to take it further when my cell phone buzzed. It was a text message from Octavia saying she'd be home soon and that she'd gotten off work early.

"Damn, Girl, look at you; that shit was good. We definitely got to do that again."

"And we most definitely will. But trust, you not ready for me," she toyed with me as she walked away toward her room.

A few moments later, in walked my girl Octavia with a huge smile on her face. She walked over to me and gave me a huge hug and kiss.

"How was your day? Are you and Cynthia getting along alright?" she questioned.

I chuckled to myself silently. "Yeah, we're getting along fine. How was your day?" I asked to change the subject.

"It was great. I can't wait to become a doctor. I get to meet so many awesome people," she replied enthusiastically.

Octavia was a good girl with a decent head on her shoulders. But boring as all hell. All she talked about was school and work. Now that Cynthia was in the picture, I had no need to stick around and pretend anymore. I just had to find a way to make my exit plan. I didn't want to make it obvious that I was on my way out of her life. I didn't want her to see it coming. That was the best way to go because she'd never expect it. I'd leave her wondering what the hell happened.

Octavia started to prepare dinner for us. In walked Cynthia giving praise to her as if she weren't just blowing me off a little while ago.

"Girl, I'm so proud of you for going to medical school and completing your residency. I just got the news that I'll be working for the state of New Jersey. So, it looks like I'll be living here in the city permanently. They're going to hook me up with a company car and assist with housing," Cynthia bragged.

"Cynthia, that is so good! I'm so happy for you. Yeah, you can stay here until everything is settled with your new job."

"It should only be a couple weeks."

Octavia ran over to Cynthia and gave her a hug. She was a good friend to Cynthia. Too bad it was not reciprocated.

It had been a little over a week and Cynthia and I were still messing around when Octavia wasn't home. I couldn't help it. This girl was like a breath of fresh air. The best pussy was new pussy.

I laid on the bed in my boxers viewing a football game. My attention was interrupted by Cynthia standing in the doorway topless. The only thing I thought of was how fast could I get her in the bed.

"Damn, Cynthia. It's like that?" I smiled.

"You not surprised. This ain't the first time we've done this," she replied walking over to the bed, taking off her panties.

This girl was forward like a m-f-'er. She inserted my dick in her pussy, no condom. Cynthia started riding me like a horse. Hearing the moans and squeals of this girl made me want to hit her harder. Every time we fucked, I felt like a new man. Sex was my drug and I'd been cold turkey for damn near a year. But the taste of this heroin was a feeling that I hadn't had in a while.

Unfortunately, this was short-lived, while this girl bounced on me, in walked Octavia, furious.

"What is going on here!" she yelled.

"Cynthia, what the fuck are you doing? I heard your ass all the way in the living room. How could you do this to me? Jeff, y'all need to get the fuck out!"

Me and Cynthia dressed fast as hell. Octavia walked away, disgusted. A few moments later as we walked toward the living room, I decided to break the news to Octavia.

"You know what, O. This ain't working out," I stated coldly.

"What do you mean it's not working out?"

"Just like I said. This shit whack. I'm bored. All you do is work and go to school. You're boring. You don't give up no ass. You honestly, think I'm going to stay with you? Girl, you got to be playing yourself."

"So, you going to leave me for Cynthia?"

"Look, she got shit that you don't have. She's thick, she's fucking, she's more interesting than you. Come on girl, get the hell out of here," I retorted.

At that point, I really didn't care how I was hurting her. I could tell this began to eat at her. But I was a playa. I didn't give a damn about neither Octavia nor Cynthia. Cynthia was just the next girl in line that came into the picture. The next chick who would take care of me and give me what I need.

"So, you're going to just walk out of my life like we never had anything?"

"What did we ever have?" I laughed at her.

"You just let me live here for free. You're the dummy," I rolled my eyes at her.

"Come on, Jeff. We got to go," Cynthia said, leading me to the door.

I had no need for Octavia anymore. Cynthia started her new job finally. She was given a company car, a house and excellent pay. What the hell did I need Octavia for. I had a chick who was working, fucking, and doing everything I needed her to do. I was a king. Everything was always about me.

Chapter 9

Octavia's Revenge

"Bitch, I told you to stop calling this phone. He doesn't want to talk to you. He doesn't want you no more. Now let me get back to your...oops. I mean, my man," Cynthia spewed and then ended the call.

How dare that tramp answer his phone. She had absolutely no remorse for her actions. Apparently, our ten-year friendship meant nothing to her. I was tired of crying and tired of feeling broken. There's absolutely no way in fucking hell that I believe this just happened. I come home from a long day after being at work and school just to find my so-called best friend bouncing on my boyfriend's dick. Then his punk ass had the nerve to tell me I never meant shit to him. As if everything we had was in vain; for nothing. All the food I cooked, all the money I gave him was all for nothing. I allowed them to leave my house that night because I surely wasn't ready to catch a charge for killing anyone. But anger enraged my heart and soul. I never saw this coming. I thought our relationship was going well only to be blindsided like this. Distraught with pain, I soaked my pillows that evening.

The next day, I couldn't believe he'd ignored all my attempts to find out what was going on. I had to get my revenge. I refused to let this mess go.

I hopped in my car and drove to Cynthia's home later around midnight. I knew she wouldn't be home. I sat in my Honda Accord parked a little further down the street. I put my gloves on and walked over to where the back of the home was. I saw an open window near the kitchen and lit an M-80 firecracker and tossed it in the window. I ran as fast as possible, back to my car, laughing all the way.

Watching the house burn up in flames gave me a slight sense of validation. Cyn came to take everything I had. She was always a jealous bitch, but this was the last straw. I deserved to get my revenge. Someone must've called the fire department. I heard the faint sound of a fire truck ring out in the distance.

Close to about an hour later, I saw them pull up next to the house. Cynthia ran out of the car screaming and yelling as the firemen attempted to extinguish the flames. Seeing the pain and agony this caused Cynthia gave me all the vindication I needed. I drove off into the midnight air without a care in the world. She could have that dude. The karma she was going to face in the future was worth more than my broken heart.

Chapter 10

Jeffrey- Playing Both Sides

When me and Cynthia pulled up to the house and saw it engulfed in flames, there was absolutely no question who could've done this. I'd been living guilt free with Cynthia for a few weeks now. After seeing this though, I immediately felt a pain in my gut. As soon as we got out of the car, I heard the wails of Cynthia screams. Luckily, the fire department arrived there in enough time to save the structure. Only the back of the house had been severely damaged. Cynthia was told she'd have to stay in a hotel until the insurance paid for the damages done to the house. Although all this shit stemmed from breaking Octavia's heart, something in me had to see her again. I realized she really did have genuine love for me. I don't know what I was thinking, but the next week, I knocked on her door hoping she'd answer. There she was, standing right in front of me, looking beautiful as ever.

"Jeffrey! What the hell do you want? Why aren't you with Cynthia?" she yelled as I dodged her hand, aiming toward my face.

"Hey look, I'm so sorry! Right now, Cynthia's up in a hotel until things get fixed. Look- "

"Good, go back to that bitch!" she screamed, attempting to close the door.

I stepped in the way. "All this made me realize is how much you really did love me. I really did love you. I truly do and I admit my mistake."

"Stop with all that bullshit, Jeffrey."

"No, no, no come on, Octavia. We've been though way too much to just throw it all away. Give me another chance and I promise I'll do right by you. I apologize. I'll never hurt you again. Please believe me," I said, winning her over.

I slowly began kissing her. I was going to get her to take me back by any means. I could tell Octavia was giving into me.

"You've got to be kidding me, you think I'm going to take you back after you broke my heart, cheated on me with my best friend and walked out on me. I thought we really had something going on and you pulled a complete 180 on me."

"Yes, Octavia I know but I sincerely apologize. I don't know what I was thinking. I made an honest mistake. But I promise if you give me another chance, I will never hurt you again. I was stupid. Cynthia didn't mean anything to me. You are the one that I truly want to be with. Octavia, I really love you. The time that I spent away from you honestly made me realize how much you truly mean to me. If you give me another chance, I can show you how I have changed. I can be the man you need. Please give me another chance. Just let me try. Please!" I pleaded with her, hoping she'd forgive me.

"We can talk about it, Jeffery. But don't expect anything…I am still watching you. You're talking a good game, but how do I know that you are telling the truth? We can talk about it…"

I wasn't expecting Octavia to fall back in love with me but hell, I needed a place to stay for a while so if I had to come back to Octavia and make her believe that I wanted to be with her again, then so be it. I had to protect myself.

A couple of months later, things were going well between me and Octavia. We were going out to the movies and out to restaurants. But just as before, she still wasn't giving up no ass. I'd received a few texts and calls from Cynthia, but I ignored her. I didn't need her right now.

Octavia sat on the bed looking beautiful. I was glad I was able to convince her to take me back.

"I'm really glad we're able to work things out. I love you, Jeffrey," she stated as she kissed my lips.

"I love you, too," I lied.

"I'm going to hop in the shower so I can get ready for my day."

"Alright, Sexy," I playfully tapped her on the leg as she walked away.

I laid down on the bed but was interrupted by the constant buzzing of my cell phone. Cynthia was blowing me up. Three missed calls, five text and two voicemail messages. I laughed at the fact this girl tried so hard to reach me because I wasn't talking to her. I didn't need her, well at least not right then. *Hmm, maybe I should answer her call. It has been two months…*

I began to get dressed, then I stepped outside the house to answer Cynthia's phone call. I couldn't risk Octavia overhearing this conversation.

"Yes, hello, Cynthia!" I replied sternly.

"What? Are you serious? I've been worried sick about you. I haven't heard from you in two months. Where are you?" she yelled.

"I'm at Octavia's," I replied coldly.

"What? Why the hell would you be with that bitch?" she questioned. I could tell I was getting to her.

"She wanted to take me back from you. You know, Octavia ain't over what happened. It was some pretty-"

"She said some things about me?"

"Yeah!"

"I'm going to fuck her up. You are mine period. Octavia knows she has nothing on me."

"She wanted to provide me with a place to stay. I didn't have any money after the fire," I lied, hoping she could give me a few things.

"Awe, I'm so sorry. I didn't know. Well, I'll be there to set her straight and my place is ready now. The insurance took care of everything. So, we got a place to stay now."

Boom! That's all I needed to hear. She gave me the red light to move forward with Cynthia. I didn't need Octavia anymore. I finally ended the call with Cynthia and went back inside.

I saw Octavia pointing to a plate of food she obviously cooked. Since I knew what was coming with Cynthia, I had to get rid of Octavia.

"Well, thank you, Babe. You're amazing."

As we ate dinner, we suddenly heard a loud banging on the door. Octavia looked upset, but I smiled like a Cheshire cat. I knew what was about to happen.

"Oh, my goodness! Who is banging on the door like this?"

As Octavia opened the door, she was greeted by a punch in the face by Cynthia. The next thing I knew, the girls were on the floor fighting.

"What the hell is wrong with you?" Octavia yelled out, holding her face.

"How you gon' take my man and put him up in your house?"

"What? He was my man first. So, what are you talking about?"

"Well he's mine now!"

"You know what, if you want him so damn badly, take him! I don't need this shit! I deserve better. The hell with the both of you. Jeffrey, get your shit and get the hell out of my house. But you know what Cynthia, you're going to face your own damn karma fooling with him. Don't come crawling back to me once he's doing the same shit to you!" she cried, as she walked away, throwing my shit out the house.

"I will never be you, Bitch!" Cynthia yelled.

Cynthia and I grabbed my stuff and walked toward her car. That was it. I was done with Octavia. But little did Cynthia know the amount of shit I was about to put her though. She wouldn't even have wanted me.

Chapter 11

Octavia's Heartache

"Ah! Get the fuck out! I hate you, Jeffrey! Fuck you and that bitch! I've been through too much bullshit with you. I don't need this shit. You get your shit and get the hell out of my life! I can't believe I thought you changed. You're always doing this shit to me. I hate you! Cynthia, you're straight bitch for what you did. Both y'all get the hell out of my house and my life."

I watched those two jerks walk out of my house and hopefully completely out of my life. I couldn't believe Jeff had set me up. Ever since I met him, my life had been one big emotional rollercoaster. One minute everything was going well between us, the next minute, we were fighting, or some drama was going down. I don't even know who I am anymore. I lost my man and my best-friend, all within a six-month time. I honestly, didn't feel any sorrow for them. Cynthia will get what's coming to her. A hell of a lot worse than I ever did. I was free. I was able to live my life. I would finish school, become a doctor and make changes in people's lives. I wouldn't have to worry about this crazy, petty drama anymore. So, hell I won the prize. Not that ho of a back-stabbing friend, Cynthia.

Chapter 12

When the Tables Turn

A year passed and things had certainly changed. Cynthia and I got married and we're expecting a baby. Yes, another woman was pregnant with my child. But as good as all this appeared, I hated this bitch. I just knew that now she wasn't going anywhere. I secured her for the long haul. Now I had free reign to roam the streets for some fresh new pussy because I knew my newly pregnant wife wasn't going to leave her husband, no matter how I treated her.

The next day after I got out of class, I sat eyes on this young lady. She always sat in front of me inside the large lecture hall. She told me her name was Aleyah.

"Hey, there Cutie. How you doing? How are you doing in class?" I questioned, just making small talk, hoping she'd give me her number.

"Oh, hey! I'm doing well. Just trying to keep up with my full course load plus work. It's pretty challenging sometimes, you know?"

"Yeah, yeah, I feel you. Um, sometimes, this econ stuff can be tough. You think me and you can get together some time and go over it?"

"Sure, that'll work. Always helps to have a study buddy," she replied, blushing and touching my shoulder.

I pulled out my phone and collected her digits. I gave her a quick hug and a kiss on the cheek before we parted ways. I was feeling accomplished, knowing I had a new girl to work on. I didn't even realize Cynthia was standing at the other end of the hallway. She looked upset, but I ignored her anyway and kept walking.

Later
That
Evening...

After we ate dinner, I hopped in the shower because I had plans on meeting up with Aleyah and it was not to study no damn econ. Of course, I couldn't tell Cynthia that. I told her that I was going to the bar with a few friends for a beer. If she were smart, she would realize I never had any guys as just friends.

As I was getting dressed, I saw Cynthia sitting on the bed going through my cell phone.

"What the hell are you doing?" I yelled, as I snatched the phone away from her.

"Your phone kept going off while you were in the shower. Please, tell me that you're not cheating on me? I am your wife and carrying your child!" Cynthia cried.

"What did you just say to me? Am I cheating on you?" I could feel the blood began to boil inside of me.

"Yes, Jeff. I see the text messages and the phone calls. I saw you with that girl last night in front of your class. If this is what you're going to be as a husband, we should just end this now."

Did this fat, stupid, bitch, just threaten to leave me? Me? Oh, hell naw! I couldn't let that happen. I had to put this chick back in her place.

"You're a stupid ass ho. Don't you remember that's how the fuck you got me! You stole me from your fucking best friend. You sucked me off the first day you met me. Fuck you talking about. And don't go through my gotdamn cell phone again!" I said, grabbing her neck and pushing her across the room.

"Don't you ever fucking question what the fuck I'm doing. It's none of your business if I'm cheating or not. You my bitch. You do what the fuck I say. Or we going to have a fucking problem. I can fuck whoever the hell I want to. Ain't shit yo' ass can do about it."

I retorted back to her after I punched her a few times in the eye and bloodied her damn nose.

"Why are you acting like this?" I heard her cry out as she covered her face which dripped in blood.

"Because I'm the mutherfuckin' devil bitch. I run this shit. Now sit yo' ass down and wait for me to come home. I'm going out for a few hours and when I get back, you better be ready to fuck or I'll beat your ass again. Do I make myself clear?"

She nodded her head in agreement as I slapped her ass, grabbed my cell phone and had Aleyah outside waiting on me.

What the hell did she expect? She wanted me so badly. She stabbed her best friend in the back to get to me. She got her wish. I guess people don't like it when those tables start to turn.

****

Aleyah and I finished studying and were sitting on her bed, making out. I began to pull back because something just didn't feel right.

"What's wrong?"

"Nothing. It's just...I was contacted from my ex and she was so cold and hurtful. It just hurts me so badly. She's abusive verbally, she cheated on me. That girl broke my heart and now I'm just afraid to get too close to any female now," I cried.

"Awe, my gawd. I'm so sorry that happened to you. But please know that not every woman is the same. I am not like that at all. I genuinely do care for you and I'll never do anything to hurt you," she reassured me.

I loved that Aleyah was so caring, so sweet, and compassionate.

"Thank you! I appreciate that so much. I really care about you."

"I care about you, too. Please know that I'll never hurt you. I can't believe your ex was so cruel to you," Aleyah stated.

These girls were so fucking gullible. I told this girl a story that wasn't even true. She ate that shit up. But I didn't care as long as I got what I wanted.

Aleyah grabbed my face and began kissing me. I laid down on her bed and allowed her to straddle me. I began caressing her gently as we undressed and started having sex. Aleyah, was so fucking sexy to me. Everywhere from her light caramel skin, her breasts and all her ass. Plus, her riding skills were on point. Man, the way this chick bounced up and down on my dick was like a workout.

We switched positions and I started pounding on that pussy. Hearing her scream and moan out my name made me cum faster. I just enjoyed getting fresh pussy. I'd been seeing Aleyah for a while behind Cynthia's back. Every time we were alone, we went at it. I basically had the best of both worlds. I had a wife and a side chick. I could get my needs met with both these hoes.

Aleyah was addicted to me. I burrowed my head in between her legs and ate her pussy like ice cream. She screamed and started squirming all around, begging for me to stop after she climaxed. I always made sure she was completely satisfied before I left her. Meanwhile, with Cynthia, I gave her whatever energy I had left.

****

Later, the next morning around 6am, Aleyah, dropped me back off at home. I walked into the house to see Cynthia sitting on the bed looking upset.

"Not now, Cyn. I'm tired."

"Tired from what? You've been gone all damn night. I was calling and texting you all night. Why didn't you answer me?"

"Cyn, I was hanging with my friends. I already told you. My buddy got too drunk and couldn't drive home. So, I waited to the next day to catch the bus home. Stop tripping. You know I love you," I lied, kissing her on the forehead.

"I love you, too. I just worry about you, Jeff."

"I'm so glad that you are so sweet and caring. I'm so lucky you're my wife," I said to get her to shut up and stop questioning my whereabouts.

Shit let me cheat in peace. I sat on the bed beside her and slowly caressed her breasts. I undressed her and entered her from the back. She groaned with pleasure. I placed my hands on her hips and fucked her hard from the back until I came. Sex with Cynthia was merely to benefit my pleasure. But with Aleyah it was new, so I had to get her addicted to me. Cynthia laid on the bed and I hopped in the shower. She was so naïve, never expected a thing. I truly had my cake and ate it too. I didn't plan on changing things up any time soon with neither one of these girls.

Chapter 13

Old Habits Die Hard

"Let's look at all the sexy women out here today!" one of my buddies said as we sat on the bleachers watching the college football game.

"Yeah, yeah, they are looking good," I commented.

"But I know you not looking at none of these ladies, since you got Cynthia," my other friend replied.

While we were talking, Aleyah walked past with one of her friends.

"Hey, what's up Jeffrey?"

"Hey, sexy. I'll catch up with you, after the game," I said to her as I playfully tapped her thigh. Watching her walk away, one of my boys, tap me on the shoulder.

"Dawg, you not..."

"Ah, Man, ain't nothing wrong with a man having options!" I laughed.

After the awful game, I parted from my buddies.

"Truman, always get their butt kicked. Alright, y'all, I'm going to see if I can catch up with Aleyah."

Making my way down the bleachers, I pulled out my cell phone to text her when I bumped into someone.

"Hey Man, watch where you're going."

When I looked up, my anger subsided. It was a familiar face.

"Jeffrey!"

"Stacy! What? Long time no hear from. You blew us out, but Truman weak anyway. Nice to see you still playing ball."

"Yeah, I'm about to go pro. It's good to see you. We going to have to catch up sometime. Let me give you my number."

Stacy and I exchanged numbers and planned to meet at the Lux Bar the following weekend.

Later That Weekend...

The crowded bar smelled of cigars, beer and nachos. Stacy and I knocked back a few beers as we reminisced on old times.

"So, how have things been? Haven't seen you since Chadsey High!" I exclaimed.

"I've been great. Me and Veronica finally did our thing," he said, flashing a wedding band on his finger.

"Same here. I married a girl named Cynthia. What team you going to?" I questioned, digging into my nachos and sipping my beer.

"Don't know yet. Could be, Broncos or Cowboys, but I'm hoping it's the Seahawks."

"Man, that's what's up! I wish you all the best."

"Thanks, Bruh! You know I miss our old hangout sessions. We got to get together real soon," Stacy said, taking a drink from his beer.

****

A couple of weeks later, I'd been seeing both Aleyah and Stacy, behind Cynthia's back. While I was getting dressed, my phone

70

went off as I turned to look at who called, thinking it was possibly Stacy, Cynthia intercepted, grabbed my phone and ran into the bathroom.

Immediately, I jumped up banging on the door. "Open the door, Cynthia. I'm not playing games with you. You better give me back my phone. I'll fuck you—"

I decided to calm down because that was not going to make her come out of the bathroom.

"Alright, Cynthia. I'm sorry, Baby. I shouldn't yell at you. You're pregnant with my baby. I'm sorry for everything I've done."

"You got to stop cheating! I can't take this anymore!" Cynthia yelled from behind the bathroom door.

"Let's work things out, Baby. I love you," I threw out there, knowing this would be the very thing that got Cynthia out of the bathroom.

"Can I have my phone back now?"

She threw me my cell phone and walked past me to the living room. I pulled her down by her hair and slap her across the face.

"Didn't I tell you to stop touching my damn phone? Why the fuck don't you listen to me, stupid bitch!"

She ran into the other room but tripped and fell.

"I shouldn't have to keep telling you, the same thing over and over again."

I socked Cynthia in the face a few times as she cried out in pain.

"Why do you do this to me? I don't deserve this!" she cried out.

"Bitch, who gon' want you? Ain't no man going to want your fat, pregnant ho ass. No man is going to want to take care of another man's baby. So, where the hell you going to go?"

I kicked her a couple times in the stomach. I knew she was pregnant, but I didn't give a fuck.

A few moments later, Cynthia screamed. I turned to see her holding her stomach while lying in a pool of blood.

"Damn, now you are bleeding on the carpet! Get up! Get your ass up!"

"I need to go to the hospital!" Cyn warned.

I'd gone too far. Pushed her into a miscarriage. I didn't want to take her to the hospital because I knew I'd get questioned about what happened and I couldn't have that. I helped Cynthia get into the shower to wash the blood off and helped her back into the bed. But I knew that I had to help her, so I dropped her ass off at the clinic and then I left to see Aleyah.

"Jeffrey, where are you going?"

"Out!"

"When are you coming back?"

"When I'm ready."

The next week, I finally came back home. Cynthia sat down at the dinner table staring at me.

"What, Woman!"

"I can't take this shit anymore, Jeff. The lies, cheating...the abuse. I deserve better than this. You've hurt me so much. I don't know how much more I can take."

I looked remorseful because things were getting out of hand. I had to be honest with myself, I was no longer interested in being in this marriage. The spark or the love that I thought I had for Cynthia had worn off. I'd gotten everything I wanted out of her. The time had come for me to move on to the next best thing I knew, and to me, that was Aleyah. I was desperate to end things with Cynthia by any means necessary.

"I have something very serious to tell you. I'm sorry, Cynthia! I really am. But um...I just found out...I got another woman pregnant. I'm so sorry. I'm so sorry."

Cynthia's mouth dropped wide open. She swiftly walked over to me and slapped me roughly across the face. I didn't retaliate because I knew what damage I caused. I was wrong.

"Are you serious? How dare you tell me that? Right after I lost our baby. You tell me there's a woman out there carrying your seed? How cruel can you be? You're so damn sick!"

She walked away toward the bedroom in tears. Honestly, Aleyah wasn't even pregnant. I just wanted to mess with Cynthia's head a little bit.

Chapter 14

Cynthia's POV: The Grass Isn't Greener

Hearing the devastating news that Jeffrey was about to father another woman's baby hit me like a ton of bricks. I couldn't believe he would stoop this low to hurt me. I simply couldn't take the abuse anymore. I was tired of moping around the house while he was out doing God knows what with God knows who. I decided to go out to the market to get what us women call, comfort food. Ice cream, cookies, etc, the works. Walking down the aisle with the store provided hand basket, I spotted Octavia pushing a grocery cart with a guy I assumed to be her new boyfriend.

"Why, hello! Funny seeing you here?"

"Why? It is the grocery store?" Octavia replied, walking away.

"Octavia, can I speak to you for a moment?"

"Talk? I'm busy, as you can see. I'm with my boyfriend. What, you want to steal him too?" she said, rolling her eyes.

"Um, no, go ahead, talk. I'll finish shopping, Octavia," her boyfriend said.

He was a tall caramel skin man with good wavy hair.

"Thanks, James. What do you want?" she asked, turning to me. "I mean, because honestly, we don't have anything to talk about?"

"I just want to say I'm sorry. I'm sorry for everything. I shouldn't have treated you that way. You were my best friend and I let a man get in between our friendship," I sadly admitted.

"Look, you wanted him. You got him. You win. I saw the pictures of the wedding and the baby news online. Congratulations. Can I go now?"

"That's what I want to talk about. After we got married everything changed between us. He changed...he changed, Octavia. He became verbally and physically abusive. He broke my nose, almost broke my leg. I suffered a miscarriage due to the abuse he put me though. I just found out he has another woman pregnant. I just can't take this anymore," I regretfully admitted as tears streamed down my eyes.

Octavia began clapping her hands and planted a smirk upon her face. I was taken aback by her reaction to my pain.

"Girl, are you serious? You want sympathy from me because now he's treating you like shit. And, oh my gawd! I can't believe he cheated on you. So surprising...not!"

"Look, I know I was wrong but Octavia, no woman deserves this..."

"No, but you tried to fight me, for him. You were wrong. I told you that you'd face your own karma. Oh, and there it is. I'm sorry he's hurting you. But you can't really expect me to care, do you?"

"We used to be best friends..."

"You are hilarious! Yes, used to, is a past tense phrase. Meaning not anymore. Enjoy your happiness. I'm sorry but you deserve whatever the hell he gives you. Now if you don't mind, I have a wonderful man who is also going to be a doctor just like me; and we need to finish shopping. Bye, Cynthia."

I watched as Octavia walked away toward James. A small tear ran down my cheek. Although, Octavia was cold toward me, I had to admit she was correct about everything she said. I did deserve the hell he put me though. I just didn't know how much more I could take from him.

Chapter 15

Jeffrey's Secret: It All Comes Out

"The NFL Draft and the Seattle Seahawks first round pick is Stacy Monroe for quarterback." The announcer yelled as Stacy walked excitedly to the stage and the crowd cheered. Veronica stood up and cheered along with them. He now realized his dreams were finally coming true. Stacy grabbed his cap and jersey while smiling for pictures.

"How do you feel being the first-round draft for Seattle?"

"It feels great! My dream is finally coming true. Now I can support my family and make Seattle proud!" Stacy replied to the exuberant sports reporters.

Later That Weekend...

I couldn't believe my boy had made it to the pros. I watched his event on TV. I hollered all the way through. Being the good friend that I am to Stacy, I decided to throw him a house party. We were drinking and smoking, and the girls were looking sexy tonight. Cynthia was out of town, so I decided to get things popping.

I looked around for Stacy at the party. He told me he wanted to turn things up a bit. The next thing I knew, me and him were in the bedroom getting it in. I had Stacy bent over the bed, hitting it from the back. Hearing the moans and groans took me to another level. Staci was, and still is, my favorite lover. Not selfish at all. Staci always returned the favor. Staci began to lay me down on the bed and proceeded to give me the best blow job I'd ever received. Shit felt so damn good. I forgot all about the party. I had to get Stacy back down on this bed, just making him moan was like being on cloud nine. I enjoyed giving it to Stacy so much, I didn't realize we were about to get caught. Suddenly, in comes Cynthia, busting through the door. I thought her ass was out of town. She must've lied.

"Jeffrey, what the hell is going on here?"

Me and Staci stopped immediately. Staci got dressed and walked past Cynthia.

"If you tell anybody about this, I will fucking kill you. I just got drafted to the pros and I don't need this shit getting out," Stacy said as he exited the room.

Cynthia stared intensely as she walked up next to me.

"I have put up with more than my fair share of bullshit from you. From the cheating, the disrespect, the abuse. Hell, even the HIV. Yes, Jeffrey, I knew! I was pregnant with your child. Of course, I knew about it. I didn't have this shit until after I got with you. And you didn't even have the balls to tell me you had this shit. Now to catch you screwing another man! I am done! I am fucking done! I want a divorce. Please just get out. Get these people the hell out of my house. All these damn women in here and you in here messing with a whole damn man!"

After Cynthia told everyone to leave and it was just the two of us alone, I let her have it. I grabbed her by the throat to make sure she heard every word I said.

"Bitch, what are you talking about? I'm not giving you a fucking divorce. You can talk all this shit if you want but where are you going to go? What man is going to want your ass now? If you walk away from this marriage and tell another dude what you got, he's not going to want you. Stop playing your damn self. Now go clean this shit up and you bet not say shit about Stacy or I'll kill you my fucking self!" I threatened as I shoved her body on the floor.

Chapter 16

Stacy's POV: A Broken Relationship

I couldn't believe Cynthia caught us in the act. I threatened that bitch not to say a word. Do you know what something like this could do to my image? I have a $50 million contract on the line here. Plus, not to mention the effect of this on my wife. Jeffrey promised me she wouldn't rat us out. Or else I'll kick his ass myself. There would be no way in hell I'd let Veronica find something out like this. This would end our marriage and my career.

Two Months Later...

We were playing the Dallas Cowboys and I was ready. This was my fifth straight win with the team since I started; so, I was pumped and full of adrenaline as I heard the roars of the crowd from the stadium. Couldn't wait as I stood in that pit running out to the field. Just as I was tossed the ball, I ran like a bat out of hell on my way to another touchdown, straight to the end zone. Nobody could touch me. I was on fire tonight. Another win for the team tonight. We kicked Cowboys ass. Feeling the full course of the momentum of the win, the team and I were shouting, hooting, and hollering. We didn't even notice the coach enter into the locker room. I went to gather my belongings to take a shower when the coach walked over and gave me some pretty shocking information.

"Hey, hey, Stacy, great win for us tonight. Your head was really in the game tonight. I appreciate that."

"Thanks, Coach."

"Yeah, but I'm sorry to tell you this but your wife, Veronica has been rushed to the hospital…"

"Oh, my gawd! Where is she? What's wrong with her?"

"I'm not sure. She passed out. She's at Lake Memorial Hospital," my coach answered me.

I ran out of the locker room and left the stadium. The thought of losing my wife almost killed me.

Later That Day...

made my way to her room. The doctors walked over to me, trying to push me away.

"That's my wife! That is my wife in there. I need to know what is going on!" I demanded.

I didn't care that people were looking at me. I needed to get to my wife. Finally, a nurse with pink scrubs on let me in the room. She told me that she passed out and needed to be monitored for several hours. I cupped my hand to my mouth and held my wife's hand. Nothing could prepare me for what the doctors told me next.

"I'm so sorry to tell you this, Sir. But we ran some test on your wife and it appears that she is HIV positive. Unfortunately, it seems to be progressing rapidly into the auto immune deficiency syndrome," the doctor said as he placed his hand on my shoulder.

"What are you talking about, Doc?"

"Your wife has AIDS."

"No, no, no! Not my wife. There's a chance I can lose my wife! No, this can't be."

I walked over to Veronica and lay my head on her chest. She looked so weak lying there in that bed. I wanted to help her, but I couldn't. Helpless is exactly how I felt.

"Sir, would you like for us to test you as well? I mean, I know that's the last thing you may want to hear but after a situation like this and by her T-cell count being so low, I have to question..."

"You have to question? You think I gave this to her?"

"Sir, I'm not saying anything and please keep your voice down. We're just looking out for her best interest as well as yours. I think getting you tested would be ideal to prevent something like this from happening to you. Now we're going to do the best we can to keep your wife healthy but if we can stop this..."

"Fine, test me."

I went along with the doctors to test me. I knew there would be nothing that they'd find. So, my only question was how the hell did Veronica get this shit? I know she wouldn't have cheated on me. Veronica was too in love with me for that. There was no way I had this shit.

An hour later, I was still at this damn hospital. The doctor came back with a stressed look upon his face. That's when all the shit hit the fan.

"I'm sorry to tell this, Sir. But you tested positive for HIV as well. We may need to run further test to check your blood cells and..."

"What? You've got to be kidding me! There has to be some kind of mistake!" I panicked.

"I assure you, Sir, there is no mistake. But having this virus doesn't mean that it's a death sentence. There are drugs and treatment you can take nowadays that make the virus completely undetectable."

"Don't tell me this shit, when my wife is lying in a gotdamn hospital bed right now. How long have I had this?"

I choked up with my head aimed at the tile floor. I wanted to run. I wanted to get out of there as fast as I could. How the hell did this mess happen? I knew I was doing some foul shit. But I thought I was being careful. I guess my past came back to haunt me.

Finally, visiting hours were over and I left the hospital. I couldn't get Veronica off my mind. Seeing her so weak and frail, I had to do something. I knew what might have triggered this and I knew exactly what to do about it.

Chapter 17

Jeffrey: A Faithful Cry Out

"Reckless. Reckless. Reckless. I was living reckless!"

I shouted out rap lyrics as I made my way back home after a college party I'd just attended. That's exactly how I was living. Every other weekend, there was a party I would hit up. There wasn't a weekend where I wasn't getting drunk. I stumbled into the house. The time was around four in the morning. Couldn't believe I'd stayed out that long. Making my way to my bed, I made a beeline to the bathroom trying to make my way to the toilet. I immediately started vomiting. I get drunk every weekend, something I'd simply got used to. But when sharp pains came from my stomach and I spit up blood, that was the moment that I knew something wasn't right. I struggled to rise to my feet but when I stood, I'd fall down to my knees. I had to crawl on my knees just to make it to my bed. Something definitely wasn't right. I had to go to the ER, but I couldn't even walk.

Eventually, as I was able to sit up on the bed, I dialed 911 and waited for them to arrive.

This couldn't be happening to me right now. I went from having the best night of my life to feeling like I was on the brink of death.

I forgot I'd left the front door unlocked until the paramedics arrived. They placed me on the stretcher and asked me several questions before an oxygen mask was put on my face. The night had certainly taken an interesting turn to say the least.

Finally, once I made it to the hospital, they placed me in a room and told me to wait for the doctor here. That time, where you have to wait for the arrival of a doctor is the longest. Plus, the room so damn cold. Doesn't make any kind of sense. I groaned for what felt like twenty minutes, curled up in the fetal position. This felt like death. I didn't know what was wrong with me, but I was sure about to find out as the doctor knocked on the door. Much to my surprise, I knew this doctor very, very well.

"Well, hello, Mr. Willis. It's definitely nice to see you again. I mean not under these circumstances per se. But I'm sure you know what I mean. Tell me what the problem is? What's causing your pain?"

"Damn, it's so nice to see you too, Octavia. I guess you were serious about becoming a doctor, huh?"

"Yes, I was. I am an MD, but we're not here to talk about me. What's wrong with you?"

"I don't know. I came home after a party like I do every weekend. When I got home, I just started throwing up blood. My stomach was cramped up. I don't know what's wrong. I can't really stand up."

"Oh, it sounds like a bit of alcohol poisoning, but I won't know for sure until we run some tests."

"What type of tests?" I questioned with concern.

"A blood and urine tests. Well, maybe just a blood test. Can I have you remove your jacket please?"

I slowly took off my jacket. This was too much of a coincidence. I never thought I'd run into Octavia again. She drew some blood from my left arm and walked out the room. She then placed some saline into my arm to stabilize my blood, then I laid down on the bed. Being in this hospital made me want to never pick up a bottle of liquor ever again. It ain't never this serious. I waited twenty minutes until the doctor... well, Octavia, came back with the results.

"So, yup. It's just as I expected. You tested positive for alcohol poisoning. Ease up on the binge drinking, you are going to rot out your liver. Plus, I looked into your chart. You haven't renewed your prescription for your medication. Now, you know this is vital to your health. You need to take your meds, Mr. Willis. Or the next time you come here; you might not leave out of here. Catch my drift."

"I'm not trying to take that shit, for the rest of my life."

"Look, I know back then there was a long list of meds you needed to take. But now we can switch your prescription, to you just taking one pill a day. I'm sure that's easier for you."

"Man, this is embarrassing, talking to you about this shit."

"Look, I've seen the worst of you. That was a long time ago. I've moved on; I'm engaged, and I am very happy. Let's allow the past to be the past, okay. Now, I'm going to write you out a new prescription and we will monitor your blood and vitals overnight. For now, please drink this cup of water and take this snack. It's to raise your blood levels. Please, take care of yourself. With alcohol poisoning and you not being stable on your meds, you could easily wind up in the coroner's lab."

She gave me a mischievous grin as she handed me the water and apple slices to eat. I knew she was just loving this shit. Knowing that her ex was nothing but a screw up and had the HIV virus. It couldn't get any fucking worse than this.

A
Couple
of
Days
Later...

inally, they discharged me from the hospital, and I was feeling a hundred percent better. I promised myself I'd never drink that much again. *Hell naw!* But I still wasn't going to take those damn pills. If I was going to die, I was going out like a mutherfuckin' G! Naw, fuck that AIDs shit. I couldn't let that shit get the best of me. As I began walking down the street, I received a text on my cell.

Hey, what up, Boy! Why don't you meet me at the Sheraton Hotel? I got us a room over here, read the text on my phone sent twenty minutes ago.

I knew exactly who it was. Stacy was ready for another hook up. Yup, I was the man, and everybody wanted a piece of me.

An hour later, I met Stacy at the room. I saw Stacy coming out of the bedroom looking and smelling good. I hadn't seen Stacy in damn near what felt like six months. We were well overdue for another tryst. Walking towards Stacy, I attempted to get a hug. Stacy pushed me back.

"What's up with you today?" I questioned Stacy.

"My wife is sitting up in a damn hospital with HIV. I wonder how the hell did she get that?"

"I don't know man. That's your woman."

"Man, I'm about two minutes away from kicking your ass."

"What? You trying to say I got something to do with this?"

"Yeah, My Nigga. 'Because I got this shit too. How'd I get the shit?"

"Let me tell you something, you a straight dude sleeping with a man. Yet, you wonder how the hell you got HIV?" I asked him, irritated.

He charged at me and we began fighting.

99

"I ought to kill yo' ass. How long you had this shit? How long you had this damn disease?" he repeatedly yelled at me.

I stood up with a busted lip as blood slowly poured out of my mouth. Laughing at his pain, I answered.

"I was born with it."

"What the fuck did you just say?"

"I-was-born-with-it. You heard me. I have been living with this shit for over twenty years."

"You knew? You fucking knew? You gave me this shit. Back in high school. You-"

"You're a damn bisexual man. Wore no protection and you're surprised you got a sexual transmitted disease. Surprise! Welcome to my world."

Stacy charged at me again, yelling and screaming. "My wife is going to die because of you."

"No, my brother, because of you. You been messing around with me since we were fourteen years old. We what, twenty-four now. That's ten years. You got what you deserved man."

Stacy tried to sock me in the face again. I dodged his hand and knocked him across the floor. How dare he accuse me because his bitch is sick.

"I'm going to fucking kill you!" he yelled at me.

"You can't kill me. I'm already dead! Because I'm the damn devil."

Before I walked out of the hotel room, a big burly buff guy stormed into the room, trying to hold Stacy back from striking me.

"Hey, hey, Stacy! Come on, man, this isn't worth it. You got a whole football career to focus on. You don't need to end up in jail fighting a case over this punk. Think man, think. I don't know what's going on but if you get caught up, you'll lose everything.

The contract, the endorsement deals, everything. Let it go, Man. Let it go. Let his punk ass walk out of here, Man."

Stacy jerked away from his teammate and walked toward the bathroom to cool off. Meanwhile, the teammate told me to get out of his room. I laughed and begin walking out of the hotel. He knew what the hell he was getting into. We'd been fucking around for years. He knew what could happen by double dipping. Shit fuck him and his wife. Wasted my time by having me come down there.

As I headed home blasting my rap music down the street. I had no remorse for the shit I'd done to other people. Aah, nope, none. *Has anyone ever felt bad for me being cursed by this horrendous disease. Nope!*

Part III

Chapter 18

Aleyah - A Year Later: Rose Colored Glasses

Okay, ladies! Now tell me the truth, have you ever met someone that was just amazing all around. I mean a good communicator, fine as hell, consistent and attentive to your needs. I mean all your needs if you know what I mean. A year, a whole year passed since Jeffrey and I decided to get serious. The time spent together was amazing. He was the sweetest person I'd ever met. Jeffrey would pick me up after work and give me massages when I was tired. We'd go out all the time, movies, restaurants, bowling, etc. I'd never met anyone like him before.

But here I was, stuck at this boring ass call center job, dealing with all these nasty, rude ass customers. I couldn't wait until this day ended. Before I made my way out of the door, I was stopped by the receptionist clerk.

"Hey, Aleyah! You've got a present from a special friend today," the clerk said.

As I waked over to the desk, I received a huge surprise. He had a bouquet of roses sent to my job. I never had any man buy me flowers, let alone bring them to my job.

"Ooh, girl! Who is this that brought you flowers? He got a brother?" my nosy ass co-worker asked.

I rolled my eyes at her. As I read the note on my way out to the parking lot, I saw Jeffrey waiting on me.

"I take it that you got your flowers. I hope you like them."

"Are you crazy? I love them. They're beautiful. Thank you so much!" I said, planting kisses all over his face.

"Hey, Babe. I got something to ask you over dinner."

"You have something to ask me?" I asked as he nodded his head and flashed that sexy ass smile that made me so weak for him.

We took off driving to the Abbot House restaurant, a beautiful upscale restaurant in the suburban area of New Jersey.

"Are you ready to be seated?" The hostess questioned us as we stood in the hallway, waiting to be seated.

It was my first time being there and I could tell the place meant one thing: expensive. Everything from the golden light fixtures to the light music playing in the background. We took a seat toward the back of the restaurant and began to look at the menus.

"Aleyah, I really brought you here to ask a very important question. I wanted to ask you..."

I couldn't believe what he was doing as he pulled a small box out of his pocket and got down on one knee. *Oh no, this is not seriously happening. Could it be?*

"Will you marry me, Aleyah?"

Shocked beyond belief as everyone in the restaurant was staring at us, I began to cry.

"Yes, Jeffrey, I will marry you!" I squealed as he placed the ring on my finger. "Well, this was completely unexpected."

"I just had to do it right. I figured it was just the next step in our relationship."

"Awe! I can't believe this!" I said as I kissed his lips.

Our waitress finally came to bring us our food and congratulated us on our new engagement. Nothing was better than this moment right now, well maybe the food. My spaghetti and breadsticks hit the spot because my ass was hungry.

"Yeah, I really love you, Aleyah. I'm ready to spend the rest of my life with you, Girl. You know you're the one for me!" he reassured me as Prince's "Beautiful Ones," played over the speakers. I knew at that moment; I'd found my soul mate.

Chapters 19

Jeffrey: Secrets & Lies

Yeah, I know what you're thinking. I don't deserve Aleyah. But I was going to do whatever it took to get whatever it was I needed. And I needed to be taken care of. But before I could move forward with her. There were some loose ends that I had to tend to.

Things between Cynthia and I were looking pretty good at the moment. I even made her breakfast in bed. I mean, she was still my wife.

"You know, Cyn, I'm really glad you forgave me for all the shit I've put you through. It's just, I've never had anyone treat me and love me the way that you do; so, I don't know how to handle it sometimes," I said convincingly.

"I mean, I will always love you Jeffrey. But you can't be treating me this way. I love you...."

"I love you, too. Don't worry, I promise from now on I will treat you better. I mean, I'm trying right now. I've never made breakfast in bed for anyone."

She smiled widely as she began to dig into her pancakes, eggs, and bacon with a side of orange juice. This plan was working just as I anticipated.

"You know, my graduation is next week. I really want you to go. I have something really important to tell you."

"Oh, my goodness! That's amazing. Congratulations! What do you have to tell me?"

"I can't tell you, yet. I will tell you next week at the ceremony. But trust me, it'll be a huge surprise for you."

"I'm excited for you. It's good that you are finally making some changes in your life. I'm so proud of you!" she exclaimed, kissing me on the lips and giving me a hug.

The next week at the ceremony, I couldn't believe the day finally came because I just knew I'd never finish no damn college. Especially with all the shit I was doing. But somehow, I pulled it off. The ceremony was looking nice, packed with people everywhere. Seeing my girl Aleyah, in her cap and gown put a smile on my face. She was so happy, to be graduating right along with me. The only thing missing, was seeing Cynthia. But I think I saw her walking up to the welcome area where the families were before the commencement began.

Cynthia approached me, with a bouquet of flowers and placed a quick peck on my cheek.

"This is really great, Jeff. I am really proud of you. Look at you, finishing up college. That's a major accomplishment. I'll have to do something special for you," she replied, giving me another hug.

"Hey, Baby, who is this? Is this your sister?" Aleyah questioned walking over to me.

"Sister? Oh no, sweetheart. I'm his wife," Cynthia replied.

"His wife? What? I'm his fiancé!" she said, flashing her engagement ring in Cynthia's face.

"Jeffrey, what is she talking about?" Cynthia asked.

"Aleyah, don't worry about her. She's an old ex-girlfriend that never got over me. Everything is alright." I say, kissing her on the cheek.

"Oh, okay. I see my father trying to get my attention. I'll catch up with you later," Aleyah says, walking off.

"Jeffrey, what the hell is that about? Fiancé? Is there something you ain't telling me? I'm still your damn wife. How in the hell are you planning to marry another woman?"

"Um, yeah, remember when I told you that I had something important to tell you? Well guess what? I want a divorce," I said, pulling divorce papers out of my back pocket and handing them over to Cynthia. She looked at them and threw not only the papers at me but hit me with the flowers as well.

"You are a horrible piece of shit. Karma is going to catch up with you some day and I swear you are going to get it. I hope you go straight to fucking hell!" she yelled before she walked away.

I laughed it off and joined Aleyah and her family.

"Oh, hey, Jeff. Come hear the good news. My father decided to pass down to me our family business! I am now the owner of the Houston Dry Cleaners. Yes!" I heard Aleyah squeal.

Hell, all I heard was *cha-ching*! Yup, I knew I hit the jackpot with Aleyah. I had to marry her real quick. What's hers is mine and what's mine is mine so I think that business is mine too. It was time that I finally received my come up. Hell, I earned that damn come up.

A
Few
Months
Later...

Aleyah and I married, shortly after graduation. Her parents paid for everything. We got married in Miami and took our honeymoon in Cancun. Now we were back in New Jersey in our own little apartment. Things were going well; I'd been working with her, running the business. She dealt with the clientele while I dealt with the finances. She taught me everything about the business. I knew how much cash came in and exactly how much cash went out. It didn't take me long to concoct a plan to get me the hell out of Jersey. I had plans for bigger and better things and it certainly didn't involve staying my ass here.

I was in the office, on the computer ordering new supplies for the dryers we had to fix when in come Aleyah.

"Hey, Babe, can you stop by the bank and make a deposit? My father needs for us to make that trip so he can make the final payment to the landlord. We have to renew the lease this month. This is like the third time he's called about it. Really appreciate it if you took care of this."

"Oh okay, sure. I'll do it. No problem!" I said yawning. I was tired.

"I'll drop it off and then head home."

"Alright, sounds good. I'm going to stay here until closing and work on some things. I should be home by the latest maybe 9 p.m."

"Awe, that's so late," I whined.

"Okay, I'll try to make it seven, but I have a lot of work to do here."

"Well, let me head to the bank," I said, kissing my wife and heading out of the door.

I absolutely had no intention on depositing that shit. I had $25,000 in cash. It was now or never. Opportunities don't come by twice. I stopped by the bank and made a withdrawal from the rest of our joint account for $5,000 then I closed it. Later, I drove home, packed all my belongings, and put them in a suitcase. Completely clearing out our closets and leaving no trace of me behind, hopped in the car and took off. Honestly, had no intention of ever coming back. I had over $30,000 and was ready to leave the past behind me and make a new start.

Chapter 20

Aleyah: It All Falls Down

It was eight-thirty and I couldn't believe I finally finished things here. Running a business was a lot of work but I knew if my father felt that I was responsible enough to handle things, then I knew I was too. As I was grabbing my belongings and heading out of the door, I received a phone call from my father. I wondered what he wanted.

"Hey, Papa. How are you?

"Aleyah. What happened to you today? I thought I told you to deposit that money. Do you want us to lose that space? It was the last payment before I finally owned that building completely. You dropped the ball, Baby Girl."

"No. no. We took care of this. I don't know what you're talking about."

"Un-uh. That money didn't get deposited today. The owner said he didn't get anything. Are you sure you went to the right place?"

"What? Yes. We do this every month. I had Jeffrey handle this."

"Well, you may need to have a talk with your husband. We need to deposit that money before the end of the month, or we will be in default. I'm serious, Aleyah. I gave you this company because I thought you'd be able to handle it. Now, I don't know if I made the right decision."

"I'm so sorry, Papa. I will handle this and get right back to you."

"I hope so," he said before hanging up.

I couldn't believe this shit. My father rarely ever got upset with me. I'm his princess and I grew up spoiled. So, when he gets frazzled, it's rare and I know that it is something very important. I drove home with hope of talking to Jeffrey to see what happened. Usually, he is on top of things. I had no idea why he dropped the ball this time. When I stepped into the apartment, it looked empty, like he wasn't home.

"Jeffrey! Jeffrey! Jeff. Are you home?" I called out to him.

There was no answer. I pulled out my cell phone and tried to reach him, but it went straight to voicemail. I went in our bedroom to lay down, but I received a huge shock. It was completely, and I do mean completely, cleared out. Everything was gone. His clothes, his shoes, his jewelry, and even the watches that I bought. Shit was gone. It didn't look ransacked or anything. Just empty. I searched the entire apartment for the money, but it wasn't there. I searched over and over. It was gone. I had a funny feeling to check our bank accounts. I saw I received a couple of emails saying that they had been closed. *Closed?* I couldn't believe it. He ran off with our fucking money. He took everything. He married me for money and left me high and dry. I was fucked. I had to come up with that money quick, fast and in a damn hurry. My father was going to kill me once he heard about this shit. I had no idea on how to break the news to him. But I had no other choice. I was in utter disbelief.

I swallowed my pride and called my father.

"What do you mean? He took everything. I can't believe this. Calm down, calm down Aleyah. We're going to handle this. This isn't your fault. I know, I know. Don't worry. We can trace the money. I have insurance for things like this. He won't get too far. I didn't last in this business for twenty plus years by not having back up plans. I'm just sorry that this happened to you, Baby Girl."

"I can't believe this. I just feel so duped. I can never repay you for this. I'm so sorry. I'm not going to rest until you get all of your money back. I'm going to come over right now so we can call the police," I said. Things were crazy right now. I couldn't believe I trusted that fraud.

Chapter 21

Getting Away with It

"Reckless. Reckless. I'm living reckless," I rapped in the car driving down the freeway, making my way to New York city.

By now, I was sure Aleyah knew that I along with the money were completely gone. I pulled off the biggest scam in history. We were married barely a year and I disappeared. There was no trace of me, nor my whereabouts. She couldn't even begin to look for me. I had everything I needed to make a better life for myself. That was exactly what I planned to do. Did I feel bad for Aleyah? That girl came from money, so she wouldn't miss that little chump change I took. I fucked up a lot of lives back there. But nobody ever cared about the fucked-up things I had to deal with growing up in my life. My father said take no prisoners. He taught me to not give a damn about anything or anybody. That was how I lived my life. It was the only way to live life. Dog eat dog world. Survival of the fittest.

As for Cynthia, she wanted a divorce anyway. Chick got what she wanted if you ask me. Stabbed her best friend in the back to be with me. Then wanted to complain about the way I treated her. Sounds like she got what she deserved. Why would I feel bad for her.

Stacy, on the other hand, knew what he was doing when he first started messing with me. You can't be a straight man then turn around and mess with a man then wonder how you caught HIV. Now he wanted me to feel sorry because his wife was sick in the hospital. He put them in that situation. Living the downlow lifestyle is a risky life. He knew what it was back in high school.

I made my exit off the freeway and continued to drive down the street, blasting my rap music. I noticed at the last minute that a train was coming. As I tried to stop the car, the brakes failed. Drivers around me started honking at me. I was stuck on the tracks. I nervously, began fidgeting with the seat belt trying to get out my car. It wouldn't release. The train got closer and closer, with every bell that rang and whistle that blew, my stomach tightened. Finally, releasing the seat belt. But then for some reason, my driver's door wouldn't open. All I could do was try to climb over to the passenger's side door. But the train just got too close...

Chapter 22

Geneva: Coming Full Circle

"We are live at the scene where a city transit train has collided with a Honda Civic on the train tracks, causing the car to explode on impact. It appears as if the driver might have gotten trapped inside of the car when the brakes stalled. Police investigators are still working on the scene. More details on this ongoing case with News 40. I'm Geneva Willis." I reported.

After my report was over, and the cameraman walked away, I walked back over to the accident scene. I saw the paramedics put the body on the stretcher. I took a closer look and dropped to my knees once I realized who it was.

The cameraman came back over to me and told me it was time to go back to the studio, but I couldn't even stand up straight.

"Hey, what's wrong, Geneva? It's time to head back to studio, producer just called."

"I can't. I can't. That's my brother. I just reported on the death of my own brother!" I cried.

"Oh, my goodness. I'm so sorry," Tim, my camera guy said.

He helped me back to the van as he drove us back. I didn't know how I would continue to follow-up with this story. I had to talk to my producer.

Walking into the newsroom, I saw Paul typing away at his desk as he looked at the monitor, prepping for the evening newscast.

"Hey, Geneva. How was that story? Such a tragedy what happened. You looked great though."

"Yeah, Paul. I need the rest of the evening off."

I saw the frightened look flash across his face. "Why?"

"The guy I reported on was my brother. I just can't... My mind isn't in the right place."

"Yeah, yeah, sure. I completely understand. I'll get Maria to fill in tonight. You know, Geneva, take the rest of the week off. I can't imagine what something like this must feel like," Paul says offering support.

"Thank you, Paul for understanding."

I talked to a couple more anchors and producers about the change in tonight's show before I left. Driving to the morgue to see Jeffrey, all I could do was wonder who'd hurt my brother. I always told my brother to watch his actions. All through high school I told him his careless ways would come back to haunt him. All he did was laugh at me. Now he was in a body bag. It's not really a question of who... but a question of whom as in which one. Who'd cut his brakes? It wasn't an old car; the brakes should have been in good condition. The brakes were clearly cut. Who'd want him dead? He made so many enemies, there was no telling who could have done this to him. I just wished his life would have turned out differently.

Epilogue

Dead... I died. That's right, my life was over but was it really? Just like a Phoenix, I shall rise from the ashes to soar again, preparing to take flight. You may kill my body, but never my soul. My spirit lives on through the lives I've infected.

I knew this day was coming soon. I'd made a lot of enemies over the years. A lot of people might have wanted me dead. I ruined a lot of people's lives with the selfishness of my ways. I prayed for forgiveness as I awaited my fate. Take it from me ladies and gentlemen, don't play with people's lives and emotions. This could very well happen to you.

Just like my father, I lost my life giving away this monster to everyone I met. Simply, because I was resentful for having been born with HIV.

Watch yourself people, anything can change and your life could be gone forever...But just like a phoenix rising from the ashes, I will rise again! I will rise again!

To see other novels from Author
Janae Marie, visit:

https://janaemariebooks.com

Leilani's Secret

Leilani's
Secret

I was coming home from another long night of rehearsal of, Fighting Back, the current Hollywood movie that I was working on. The rain and thunderstorm worsening as I turned to pull up the driveway. Luckily, I had my umbrella lying in the back seat. I checked to see what time it was, and my digital clock read to me: 1:15 am. I could not believe that the time had flown past like that. I hoped Leon was still sleeping so I could sneak into the house, unnoticed.

I turned off the ignition to my Porsche, grabbed my umbrella and walked toward the porch. I fumbled through my purse to find my house keys. I finally unlocked the door and stepped into the house. Looking around a bit startled, it was darker inside the house than outside. I tried to reach for a light switch and the next thing I knew, I heard Leon's voice pounding from the end of the hallway as I saw a tall figure running toward me. I slid against the wall as I anticipated what would happen next.

"What the hell are you doing coming home so fucking late, Leilani?" he asked, yelling at me.

"Leon, you knew I had rehearsal tonight. I just did not expect it to last so long. Sorry, I lost track of time. But it is not the first time, so why are you always trippin'?" I stated as I tried to plead my case.

"That's just it, shit! I'm tired of you coming home so late all the damn time. What the fuck are you doing that you have to keep coming home so late? Are you cheating on me? You're cheating, aren't you?"

"No, Leon. I am not cheating on you. I don't have time to cheat any damn way."

"What? So, you are saying if you had the time you would?"

"Leon, you're taking it the wrong way, you know what I mean. I'm tired; I don't have time for this. I just want to go to sleep."

"Hell no, forget that! I'm not letting you get away from me that easily. I'll be damned if you cheat on me and think you can get away with it!" he repeated over and over.

"I'm not cheating on you! What the hell is wrong with you? I was at work! Why do you always think someone is cheating on you? Are you cheating on me? Do you feel guilty for some stupid shit that you did? Now you just want to blame that shit on me. I'm tired of this, Leon. Damn..."

"I don't know who the fuck you think you're talking to like that!" he said as the thunder clapped and the rain poured down even harder.

It was one thing to be arguing but I don't think the weather helped the situation. The more the thunder boomed, the scarier it made Leon's voice appear to be. I just wanted this night to be over. But it was far from being done.

I walked past him toward the stairs; I didn't want to argue with him tonight. He knew I'd never cheat on him, so I didn't know where all this was coming from. I just wanted to crawl into bed and get a good night's sleep. Well, a good morning's sleep. But he just wouldn't let this go.

"No! I'm not letting you walk away from this shit!" he said, as he pulled me from my waist and threw me onto the floor.

I tried to rise to my feet, but he started to punch me in the face. I blocked my face with my hands and kicked him in the groin. I tried to run to the den as fast as I could to escape from Leon's treacherous fit. *Here we go again*, I thought. I couldn't take coming home to his abusive ways. I did not need this. I sure as hell did not deserve this. Every night we fought. Every night we argued, every night I'd end up bloodied and bruised. Every night he'd lie as he looked me in my eyes and told me that he loved me. Every night I'd cry as I felt that each day another part of me died.

"You bitch! Wait 'till I get my hands on you. I'm going to kick your ass!"

"Leon! Leon, just please leave me alone! I'm tired of going through this with you. You're going fucking insane!"

"Oh, I'm the one that's insane while you're going out doing God knows what with God knows who." I sat in the den with the door locked wondering why I continued to endure this pain and misery from a man that clearly didn't love me. I knew that I deserved better, but I was just too damn afraid to leave him. I was paralyzed in fear and stuck in a loveless relationship. The house turned quiet and even the thunder stopped booming. I assumed that Leon had given up his pursuit of trying to chase me down. I slowly crept to the door and still everything seemed silent. I opened the door and walked into the hallway. I proceeded down the hall toward the downstairs bedroom. Sadly, the next thing I knew, Leon had appeared out of nowhere.

"You thought I would forget about this shit!" he shouted.

As soon as I heard his voice, I stood frozen in fear; that paralyzing feeling came over my body again. I don't know what happened next because moments later, I felt Leon hit me in the back of the head with a metal baseball bat. I fell to the floor. I blacked out. I know I could've died that night. All this shit this man has put me through. I couldn't take it anymore, so why the fuck was I doing it. This was just the tip of the iceberg. Maybe I should back up a minute and explain how everything got so rough between me and Leon. Because honestly speaking, things were not always this horrific between us. Let me tell you the story of how Leon and I first started dating. One meeting changed my entire life as I struggled to juggle college and my professional acting career. I guess love really can be deadly.

Acknowledgements

I would love to thank my family for always supporting me. Especially my daughter, Kayla, and my little, big sister, that is taller than me, Kiana!

Also, my friend Shareta Williams (she knows who she is) for being so patient and threatening me if I published another book before this one!

I really hope you enjoy this read. I truly appreciate your support.

I love you, Mom!

Much Love!